Stories by the Dozen

Stories by the Dozen

A Collection of 12 Short Stories

George Pettett

Each story in this collection is a work of fiction. Any resemblance to any person living or dead is purely coincidental.

ISBN: 1508835721
ISBN 13: 9781508835721

For those readers who asked for more.

Contents

1

The Breakfast Gang

Only two members of the customary five were present when Jerome appeared in the doorway of the big dining room. Max, seated farthest from the door, scowled at sight of the tall man who hesitated where he stood.

"Here comes your friend," Max said to Paul, whose wheelchair took much of the space at the opposite side of their table. Paul turned his head to see an attendant named Gracie point Jerome toward his assigned place.

Their ad hoc breakfast club grew accidentally, like separate mishaps which landed four of them in Shadow Springs Nursing Home and Rehabilitation Center in the first place. Max, Paul, Charlie, and Emory resided temporarily in the rehabilitation wing to recuperate from falls and similar punishment to aging bones.

The management liked to seat at least five at each round table. Alzheimer's-afflicted Jerome – a permanent resident of the nursing home – had been assigned to their table because he could walk upright and slide his chair within space left once the wheelchairs of Paul and Charlie and the walking frames that supported Max and Emory were all in place.

"Why do you try to explain?" Max asked.

"I'm not explaining anything, Max... just making conversation," Paul offered. "I know he doesn't comprehend events of the past 30 years or so. He knows classical music, though. He likes to talk, and music may be the one thing he can talk about."

All five were talkers. No subject was off limits for discussion over servings of oatmeal with sausage patties that rotated every other morning with scrambled eggs and strips of bacon on their menu. Jerome, on mornings he did not sleep through the breakfast hour, introduced classical music into the mix. Such moments cued Emory's eyes to roll, Charlie's sudden attention to the newspaper on his lap, and Max's nod of head signaling that Paul would be on his own until he managed to change the subject.

"You're a patient man, Paul," Max said, "but he doesn't understand you. Accept it."

"We... every one of us in this place," Paul said as Jerome came near, "needs someone to talk to. After you and I get out of here we'll go our separate ways and may never see each other again. But Jerome is here for the rest of his life. His fate is lonely enough. I can't deny him a listener. To whatever he may wish to say."

Jerome arrived just ahead of the nurse Raiwanna who chased after him with a small paper cup half filled with pills. He took the cup obediently and swallowed its contents with a stout swig of orange juice as he seated himself alongside Paul.

"Morning, Jerome," Paul greeted him.

Across the table, Max sipped his coffee.

"Good morning," Jerome replied as he proceeded to inspect then rearrange tableware set before him. Once satisfied with knife and fork alignment, he asked the question he asked the day before, and the day before that.

"Do you like Brahms?"

Paul was ready with his answer. "Yes."

Jerome leaned closer. "Surely you know his Concerto for Violin? And his First Symphony?"

"I like the part that goes," Paul began to hum, "Da Doom... Doom Doom Doooom Doom..."

Jerome reacted with the same blank expression given Paul's previous attempts to hum the one segment of the symphony's closing movement he could remember.

"Who conducted?" Jerome demanded, "Toscanini?" He paid no attention when an attendant named Nolie placed a plate of eggs and bacon in front of him, but the act afforded Paul time to proceed cautiously in the conversational minefield.

"Yes, I believe it was a Toscanini recording." Paul said, not wishing to claim too close acquaintance with any composer or conductor because that invited still more questions. One morning Jerome pressed for other works by Brahms with which Paul was familiar, and the Lullaby was the best he could offer. He learned to let their conversations remain one-sided. Jerome's side.

As Jerome began to tell again of his childhood in a home filled with recorded music of the masters, Max stuffed half a strip of bacon in his mouth and followed it with a bite of toast. Paul kept ears and eyes attuned to Jerome's lecture on music appreciation until sudden movement from across the table intruded.

Max's left hand slapped against the table top. A contorted expression filled his face. His chin sagged.

"Max...what's wrong?" Paul asked. He stretched his arm full length but could not reach the man who struggled to draw breath. "Gracie! Nolie!" Paul called out. "We need help over here." At that precise moment, it seemed every attendant must have retreated to the kitchen. Occupants at tables nearby did not respond.

"Jerome," Paul interrrupted the narrative about music, "Max is choking. I can't reach him from this wheelchair. Will you get up and step behind him?"

Jerome's puzzled look did not offer encouragement.

"Please...he's choking to death," Paul said. "Get behind him and put your arms around his chest. Quickly! I'll show you what to do."

Jerome stared but did not move.

"Go behind his chair," Paul tried to sound calm as his left arm pushed hard against Jerome's shoulder and right arm pointed to Max. "Put your arms around him...like this." He extended both arms to form a circle. *"Now!"*

Max's head and shoulders drooped. His arms had disappeared below the table.

Jerome left his chair and, still watching Paul, moved in back of Max.

"That's right," Paul encouraged. "Now, like this," he demonstrated, "Arms around his chest. Squeeze hard!"

With eyes fixed on Paul, Jerome bent and placed his arms around Max.

"Squeeze!" Paul shouted.

Jerome jerked the slumped man's back against the chair.

"Again! Harder!"

A second thrust sent a wad of half-chewed food flying onto the tablecloth.

"That's it...now once more!" Paul said.

A grunt sounded from the man in the straight chair when Jerome applied pressure a third time. Max's flushed face erupted into a coughing spasm that led to snorts of assurance his windpipe had been reopened.

"Good work, Jerome," Paul complimented. "You can sit down now. He's OK."

Jerome, his puzzlement unchanged, stepped away from Max's chair when the attendant Gracie rushed in to lift a water glass to Max's face. "Take some water, Mister Conway," she said. "A sip of water will stop that cough."

"Leave him alone, Gracie," Paul said. "He wants air more than water. We sure needed you, or somebody, a couple minutes ago. I called for help, but you all had left the room."

Without a reply, she scooped the lump of discharged food into a paper napkin, tugged at Max's shoulders to straighten his position, and left the table as silently as she had appeared.

"You can sit down now, Jerome," Paul said, relief evident in his tone. "You saved a man's life."

The coughs and snorts from Max faded to muffled gasps. His dazed eyes looked first at Paul whose left hand pointed to the rescuer

"Thank you...Jerome," Max wheezed as the hero of the moment reseated himself.

The gratitude in Max's eyes convinced Paul there would be no questions about Jerome's inclusion in future conversations at their table. He would rely on Max to explain it to Charlie and Emory.

2

Wrong Turns

We found a welcome inside the whitewashed stone walls of the little lochside hotel in Scotland's Argyll District.

"Our last room available," the proprietress said, "and you're just in time for dinner."

I hurried to and from the car for our luggage, leaving Alicia to supply the essential information since we arrived without a reservation.

"At last... something about this day goes right," I said as my wife preceded me up the narrow stairway.

"Did she say 'turn left at the landing?'" Alicia asked before supplying her own answer, "Yes, I'm sure she did."

I fell in behind her turn at the top of the stairs. "Surely," I puffed, "her directions are better than what we were given at that rental car counter in Glasgow."

"If you had taken the GPS like they suggested, you would not have made so many wrong turns," Alicia chided over her shoulder as she headed for the only wideopen door of five that surrounded the landing. A white ceramic number affixed to each door's face identified each of the four bedrooms. The door to a bathroom we were to share with other lodgers, left slightly ajar, bore a simple B.

"Or, if I'd been traveling with someone who knew how to read a map," I protested. "Do you realize how much we'd have paid after using that gadget for the next ten days? That would bite into your shopping for woolens and my budget for Scots whiskey." I tossed our bags atop the double bed. "Whatever, we're here now. Let's get back downstairs. They'll be waiting for us in the dining room."

After quick freshenings of face and hair, we hurried down to a deserted lobby. Our proprietress beckoned from the open doorway of the dining room. She led us to the lone unoccupied table, nudged against the wall opposite three tables aligned with tall windows affording splendid views of sunset on the loch. Alicia and I offered polite nods of apology to diners at those tables who awaited our being seated so everyone might be served the first course.

"Cullen Skink," our proprietress announced to everyone as she assisted another woman in serving each table. "Soup made using local fish."

"Delicious," I pronounced after my first spoonful.

Alicia studied our fellow diners. The table nearest her was occupied by a young couple who had not acknowledged our arrival. Their chairs were turned for a fuller view of the loch or to minimize the chance their conversation could be overheard. The man seemed to be well into some lengthy narration. His right hand emphasized a phrase now and then with a vigorous gesture. Head down, the young woman appeared to listen without looking at him or anyone else.

I sensed Alicia's determination to attract attention. She maintained a steady gaze across the back of the young woman's head as if something out on the loch demanded to be noticed.

A sixtyish man sat alone at the table closest to me. His face suggested an outgoing nature.

"Here for the fishing?" he asked me.

"No, my wife and I are rambling the Highlands for a few days before we fly back to the States," I replied.

"Bonnie notion," he said. "Weather's good for that this week. If you change your mind about the fishing, I'll be glad to have you join my gillie and me tomorrow. He'll call round for me at breakfast. Keen fellow... knows this loch, I'll tell you. He'll kit you out...guest license...all that."

I thanked him without commitment. The soup appealed to my empty stomach and soothed jumpiness brought on by an afternoon of driving misadventures. Across from me, Alicia shifted position in her chair several times but kept her eyes fixed on her target.

"Your soup's getting cold," I reminded. "It's excellent. I trust it means we can have great expectations of what's to follow."

Alicia dipped into the thick soup but glanced back at the young couple more often than she raised the spoon to her lips. To her credit, Alicia is one of the best-natured, genuinely hospitable persons on earth. But if her attempted sociable entreaty is not returned to a tiny degree at least, she doubles down in meditation about what could possibly be happening in another woman's life that curtains off what Alicia considers simple courtesy. A nod, a glance, a lifted eyebrow. Some basic show of acknowledgment, and all's well in Alicia's world. Indifference, however, frustrates her..

The object of her concentration did not look up while she ate. Her husky companion's hunched shoulders conveyed tension. He continued his monologue throughout the meal.

I happily gave in to the charms of Scottish beef slathered in its rich dark juice that testified to hours of slow roasting perfection. Before I realized it, I accepted servings of both potatoes and parsnips along with the obligatory peas that seem part of every dinner served where the Union Jack flies over all. My feast left little room for dessert, but that was overcome once I spotted the big bowl of Trifle on the service cart.

"I'm pleasantly stuffed," I sighed. Alicia had hardly spoken throughout dinner. Each bite she managed seemed to trigger another automatic glance toward the young couple's table. Even when the young man stood and shifted his weight impatiently in the aisle, the woman did not respond to Alicia's glance but simply followed him out of the room.

When our proprietress Mrs. Grant – she reintroduced herself during the serving of the courses – appeared to ask if dinner had been to our liking, I assured her of our pleasure.

"Coffee and afterdinner drinks are being served in the lounge," she said with a smile.

"Fine...we'll adjourn there now," I said and moved to Alicia's side.

"Something's not right, Dan," she whispered as I pulled her chair back from the table. "He's dominating her," she added while we walked to the bar.

"You think that.... just because that woman didn't speak to you? Come on, Alicia... you're imagining too much. Let's have a nightcap."

We moved into the compact bar that backed up to the reception area. I waited for Alicia to choose where to sit because I knew she'd wish to keep the

young couple in view. She passed up an accommo-
dating spot beside the friendly fisherman and chose
instead a cramped space that allowed her to sit with
her back to the wall and face the young woman.
That placed the young man back to back with me,
our chairbacks less than a foot apart.

Our squeezing into place afforded Alicia an
opportunity to try an apology as a means of gaining
attention.

"Please excuse us," she said cheerfully. "We hope
we haven't jostled you."

A grunt sounded from the man when I settled into
my chair after getting our drinks at the bar, but he
kept his eyes and words directed to the silent young
woman.

Alicia sighed. The look from her brown eyes traveled laserlike across my right shoulder.

"You're staring," I cautioned after a sip of Drambuie.

"They wouldn't notice," she whispered without
a blink. "Her head is scarcely above the tops of the
glasses in front of them. She hasn't looked up since
we came in. He's lost in whatever he's telling. He's so
intense. She just *sits* there, Dan. I wonder..."

"Perhaps he's recruiting her for a mission," I teased.
"James Bond stuff. Get the goods on some ambassa-
dor, or a baron of British commerce."

"I wonder if she needs help," was Alicia's way of
dismissing my suggestion. "A victim of mental abuse

may not know how to signal. It's *true*, Dan. Or a previous attempt failed... and consequences could have..."

"Please finish your cocoa," I urged. "I want to get to bed. Those narrow roads and that car got the best of me today."

"Well, I'm concerned for her even if you're not. She's so young... seems intimidated. He's so much stronger. I wish she'd look at me."

When I persuaded her to leave, Alicia insisted on circling behind me and bumped the back of the man's chair.

"Oh, please excuse me," she said. "I simply meant to say good night as we passed."

His gruff "Good Night" sounded without a word or movement from his companion.

Our entrance at breakfast found them seated already. The young woman surprised Alicia with a sunny smile and wave of hand. The man appeared gloomy by contrast. He had nothing to say while the two women exchanged polite greetings. He rushed their departure as fast as the young woman could be hurried through her toast and tea, then straight out of the hotel.

As we checked out, Alicia seized her opportunity to query the proprietress woman-to-woman.

"We couldn't help but notice," she began, "the couple who left just a few minutes ago... well, the man dominated their conversation so decidedly last night, both during dinner and later in the bar, that... we wondered... you know, whether a bystander should step in to offer her relief from such intense pressure."

Mrs. Grant concentrated on applying our bill against my credit card. She did not look at Alicia, but proof she listened came quickly.

"She seemed quite cheerful this morning, Ma'am," she said.

Alicia pounced. "That's just *it*. Such a contrast to her demeanor last night. He, on the other hand, appeared sullen this morning. Causes one to wonder if someone may have... intervened?"

"That would not be our doing, Ma'am." The proprietress returned my card with a slip for my signature.

"Well..." Alicia pressed on, "his behavior last night bordered on abuse. There are so many instances of spousal abuse now..."

"Oh, did you think they are a couple?" Mrs. Grant asked, looking straight into Alicia's eyes.

"I saw her rings..."

A veteran actress of the London stage would have envied the timing of the hotelkeeper's next remark.

"The young woman *is* married. But *not* to the gentleman you saw."

Alicia breathed audibly, uncertain of her ground of inquiry.

"He is her *brother*," came the explanation. "They're here for a few days to decide what's to be done with their late uncle's estate. Very large place nearby... in the family for centuries. I expect there's much to discuss and decide upon. He prefers to sell. She does not. Intense matter, I'm sure, but I believe she is winning."

I leaned in to accept a copy of the slip I had signed. "Thank you, Mrs. Grant. We've enjoyed our stay. Now we're off to see the heather and sample a few single malts."

I nodded for the silent Alicia to precede me to the car park.

3

The Preening Room

Fred Blankenship's voice of protest shook the quiet of the fully-lit conference room.

"Dammit! I *knew* no one would be here."

The senior vice-president of Abblet Advertising Agency yanked at a chair and took his accustomed seat at the immediate left of the yet to appear agency president's position at the head of the long mahogany table. "Meetings called for nine o'clock should begin at nine o'clock!" Blankenship removed his rimless glasses and wiped them vigorously for emphasis.

"Easy, Fred," said the younger man who followed him in and moved to the center of three chairs aligned on the opposite side of the table, "at least Laura's been in to turn the lights on for us. Save your energy til we know what this is about." Ray Culver settled into his accustomed chair and placed a yellow pad before him. Culver was the agency's creative director, but that title no longer carried its onetime significance. Essential creative policy now belonged to the recently hired California wonder boy who had been commissioned executive vice-president. That status earned Graeme Farr the privilege of appearing for staff meetings only when the president entered the room.

Blankenship had not expressed all his displeasure. "Shows no respect for people's time, that's what it does. I'm due at Citadel at ten o'clock." The older man repositioned his glasses and sought Culver's understanding. Blankenship had shepherded Citadel Bank's advertising campaigns for a dozen years. That account ranked second in importance only to Westway Airlines in agency billings.

A strikingly attractive fiftyish brunette rushed in, hands juggling a portable electronic device, a Starbuck's cup, and a brochure. She took the chair at Blankenship's left.

"Morning, Maggie," Culver said. "Had word long?"

"Ten minutes," Magdalena Luis-Garcia sighed, "text from Laura." She busied herself placing items on the table before her – cup immediate right, phone at center, brochure to her left. The agency's supervisor of account services styled her dark hair straight back above the ears, widening the intelligent appearance of her olive-hued forehead and dark eyes. Her charm and choice of outfits in rich colors made her a favorite with the brass at Westway. They ignored any suggestion for promoting the carrier's routes and service unless it carried Magdalena's personal endorsement.

"I found out on my way in," Culver said. "Fred was honored with a phone call."

Blankenship resumed his muttering. "If that's what you call a cell phone summons as you back out of your driveway, then I suppose I was honored."

A fourth member of the staff slipped in and seated himself in the chair at Culver's right. Andy Vincent did everything quietly. The agency's veteran art director spoke rarely even when questioned, opting to dash off a few strokes on the small sketchpad he always carried and offer that in reply. He was a keen listener, able to capture the essence of an idea instantly in a simple sketch.

Blankenship drummed the fingers of his right hand on the table and glanced at his watch. He marked the passing of each minute by spreading the same fingers flat before he resumed his nervous tapping. Luis-Garcia relaxed and sipped her coffee.

Culver, seated opposite the open door, saw shadows approach in the hallway and signaled the others. All four rose to standing position as Mitchell Abblet strode into the room, followed by Farr and Dorothy Burns, the agency comptroller. Burns carried her laptop to the far end of the table. Farr glided in back of

Abblet to take the right corner spot between the president and Culver.

The commander motioned for his troops to be seated.

A lightning-fast change came to Blankenship's facial expression. He beamed his best effort to appear pleased and eager to hear from his chief.

Abblet usually greeted his top staff with an ear-to-ear smile and jolly remarks. The show of ebullience was there this morning. The agency president was his impeccable, well-groomed self. However, the uncommon silence before a word was said signaled Culver that awkwardness had joined the uncertainty already present in the room.

Culver had often thought an executive recruiter obsessed with packaging would have gone looking for a Mitchell Abblet had the live specimen not been present to succeed his late father as principal of what had become Dallas's third largest locally-owned advertising agency. Mitch, as Abblet liked to be addressed, exuded confidence. He took pride in his tailoring. Tall and perpetually-tanned, with the practiced movements of an athlete, he expected eyes would turn his way and ears would heed his voice. He saw his conference room as his performance hall.

He began this meeting by recalling occasions when he assembled his agency's top guns in this room for the announcement of a new account or final polishing of a major presentation. "Landmark days," Mitch summarized. Blankenship's chin bobbed up and down in agreement at the end of each sentence. Luis-Garcia's neck and head held the classic pose of a subject's sitting for her portrait. Farr crossed his arms impatiently at his chest.

Something big is up, Culver thought.

All the staff knew Mitch relished rubbing elbows within the moneyed circles of Dallas and Highland Park, although his marginal qualification for entry came from marrying well. However, he could not bring himself to comply with conservative standards of dress favored in dark-paneled boardrooms and private clubs. Where other businessmen wore colored dress shirts with white collars on occasion, Mitchell Abblet wore one every day. He shunned pastels. Mitch's custom-made collection included sapphire, jade, ocher, salmon, and copper. This morning he had selected magenta accompanied by a purple-and-silver tie with matching pocket scarf framed in a slate-gray pinstripe suit. Heavy silver links shined on the stiff white cuffs of his shirt.

"Those were great moments," Mitch proclaimed, "under the banner of Abblet Advertising. We meet this morning under a new banner. Last night, I accepted an offer to merge with Prentiss and Welsh."

The last words brought sudden intakes of breath from most of those seated around the table. Exceptions being a bored Farr, and Dorothy Burns, who studied the screen of her laptop.

Mitch kept talking, "Locally, this office will be known as Prentiss, Welsh and Abblet."

He paused for that to sink in and leaned back in his chair.

"These things bring on a lot of duplication," Abblet resumed once he straightened to the table. "Our associates in New York and Los Angeles will now provide many of the things we have been doing in account service," he paused again. "Production and media will continue to be outsourced. Graeme will spend a lot of time commuting between New York and here. A team from the Los Angeles office will arrive this afternoon to outline services for Westway. Exciting prospects there, I'll tell you. Dorothy will remain my personal assistant here, Laura will continue as receptionist, and one junior account executive will join us soon from the New York staff." Again, he paused. "For the rest of you, I must say that your positions have been made redundant."

Culver swallowed and ran his right hand across the back of his sandy hair. He looked across the table, first at Blankenship, who appeared comatose, then at Luis-Garcia. Her proud head remained erect. She gazed at Abblet as if he were some stranger who dared to intrude in her presence. At his right, Culver sensed movement as Vincent rose from his chair and, without a word, left the table.

Before Vincent was out the door, Abblet spoke again: "Dorothy will go over stock buybacks and severance packets with you individually." He placed his palms on the table and pushed his chair back.

Blankenship regained consciousness and croaked out a question.

"Mitch…what about Citadel? You'll need me to…"

Abblet stood erect and placed a hand on Blankenship's shoulder. "You've done a wonderful job for the bank, Fred," he praised, "but I'll see that everything is taken care of."

Scrambling to his feet, Blankenship pleaded, "But the officers rely on me…"

The smiling Abblet moved toward the door. "I realize that's been the case, Fred. I'm pretty well acquainted with them, too." He shook Blankenship's hand in parting, "I'm sure you haven't forgotten the chairman of Citadel is my father-in-law."

With Farr at his heels, Abblet left the room.

Six months later:

Culver clicked "Save" on his word processor and reached for the ringing telephone.

"Ray Culver," he said hurriedly. The old business habit of identifying himself to callers continued after he swapped going to an office downtown for staying put at a tiny lakehouse a hundred miles east of Dallas.

"Ray! How are you?'

The familiar voice of Magdalena Luis-Garcia came through the earpiece. He leaned back in his chair.

"Well, Maggie...what a pleasant surprise," Culver said, smiling into the phone. "I'm glad you haven't gone Hollywood and forgotten your old friend out here in the country. How's life in big old Los Angeles?"

"I'm settling in – go where I need to go – see who I need to see – the rest can wait," she said in her customary staccato delivery. Her manner of speaking proved effective in business presentations because it established her grasp of a situation and allowed few opportunities to interrupt until she wished. With friends and favorite clients, she softened the sharpness with a lilting Latina inflection at the end of a key word or phrase.

"I had to tell you what I've just learned," Magdalena's voice became a throaty purr.

"The agency is cutting Mitch loose!"

Culver blinked. "Say again?"

"Mitch is out," she raised her voice and hurried on,. "As of this morning – no more Prentiss, Welsh and Abblet – I heard it straight from Bill."

Culver knew that meant Bill Saxton, president of Westway Airlines. When Abblet announced the merger shifted oversight of the Westway account to the Los Angeles office, the airline president intervened. Prentiss and Welsh had long been pursuers of the airline's account. Absorbing Abblet Advertising through merger was a means to that end. But the principals had not foreseen Saxton's demanding they hire Luis-Garcia, otherwise he would entertain presentations from other agencies. She joined the West Coast office straightaway but flew regularly to Dallas as part of the account team working with Westway executives.

Magdalena rushed on:

"They will keep Farr in New York. He called Bill – smug and proud of himself, according to Bill – said he'd be out here in a day or two."

Once she paused for breath, Culver seized his chance to talk.

"Sounds like the king of the mountain may have been knifed by his trusted prince," he said. "I guess Old Mitch will have to start all over, huh, Maggie? Let's see... he still has Citadel to build on..."

"Not for long," she interrupted. "Bill has heard," and her tone became whimsical, "an ex-playmate squealed – Mitch's wife found out – she's filing for divorce. The peacock won't strut when that happens."

Culver could not help laughing along with her.

"I had to tell you, Ray," Magdalena was off and running again. "Sorry if I disturbed your train of thought – your novel? – how is it going?"

"No disturbance at all, Maggie," he lied. It would take hours to clear his mind from all she told him. He worked doggedly to avoid reminiscing about his years at the agency. The move to the lake had helped, along with his decision to resume the writing of an oft-postponed mystery novel.

But hearing Luis-Garcia's effervescent voice again pleased him. Culver admired survivors like Magdalena. And Andy Vincent, who had emailed two terse sentences about becoming a partner in a small art gallery in New Mexico and happily daubing a few canvases himself. Unlike the desperate calls from poor Fred Blankenship, still clawing for a place in the Dallas advertising world.

"My brain needed a rest," Culver told her, "Haven't decided what my dashing sleuth's next move should be."

Magdalena broke in, "Well, if you send him chasing a jewel thief – into a fancy dress-up affair – make sure he gets out with all his tail feathers."

4

Happy Hour at Saucylicious Barbecue

The last shift of the lunch crowd left an hour ago. The hum of their voices has faded like the sheen gone from auto license plates tacked across interior walls of the rustic single story building. Only three tables are occupied, but spirited conversation at each one sends up comments that echo from the metal tags identify-ing a majority of states in the union and most every year since the end of World War II.

Out front on the packed clay parking lot, four pickups and two sedans announce to drivers on the interstate that midafternoon arrivals inside this haven for barbecue-lovers are welcome and expected. With choices of smoked beef, pork, turkey, and chicken come opportunities to overhear honest expressions of East Texas wisdom as enticing as aromas from the kitchen.

What matters most to three good old boys dug in at a corner table is the high school football team's upcoming game. The restaurant's slow pace after lunch encourages each man to lean back and listen when a companion speaks. Their statements, however, maintain the volume necessary when the room was packed.

"I tell you," exclaims one voice, "that boy can throw it forty yards on a line."

A table companion expresses disbelief.

"Homer, he's not but fourteen years old."

"That I don't deny," Homer responds. "But he's six foot two already, a hundred ninety pounds, and still growing. Coach needs to wake up and see the gift he's been dealt in this year's crop of freshmen."

That leads the third man of their party to chime in. "Leave him on defense this season. He fills a need in that secondary."

Homer pursues his case for upgrading the team's offense but fails to attract support or even attention from either of the two women who occupy a table farther back in the room.

"I can't imagine what's keeping Connie," a sassy voice rings clearly. "We can't decide anything about our Veterans Day program until she tells us whether that building's available."

"Yes, the *place* is a mighty necessary detail, Earline," says the woman seated with her. "The auditorium at the Electric Membership Co-op is so much roomier than the VFW lodge. It's more family friendly, too."

"It will be nice to honor our veterans someplace outside their own four walls for a change," Earline agrees. "Let me try her number again."

"Here it is midseason," barks the third member at Homer's table, "and you want to deflate the confidence of our starting quarterback, wreck the secondary, and confuse the rest of our team."

This does not deter Homer. "Wendell, you need to eat more jalapenos. Show some fight! Our running game is predictable and young Hendrix can't throw downfield. The Stallions have got to open it up to have any chance..."

"Connie? Where are you? Jo-Ella's here...we're waiting for *you*..." Earline speaks into her phone at such high pitch Homer is forced to lean closer to his companions if they are to hear his reworked game plan.

"You're *where*? All right... but hurry."

The women at the table exchange nods.

"Don't say it, Earline," Jo-Ella cautions. A capricious smile breaks the composure of her lambent African-American face. "That state trooper was reassigned, remember?"

Connie's whereabouts draws no more attention than the football analysis has stirred at the third populated table in the room. By a front window, two men sit hunched over an architectural drawing laid across a tabletop adjoining the one where they ate lunch. The older of the two sips from a bottle of Dr Pepper and grunts aloud while the younger man uses a pen to point out specific representations on the paper one by one.

"They've taken your suggestions here.... and here," the penholder says. "There's no wiggle room on the far side unless you know how to get around the railroad's right of way."

"I don't," the older man says. He sips again and scans the room to see if anyone might overhear. "Unless someone can show drainage ditches are in their best interest. Your lawyers and their lawyers would spend years debating that with the EPA, I imagine."

The younger man begins to roll the large drawing to form a tube. "Then I can report you have no further objection to our plan?" he asks.

"I didn't say that, Michael," his senior drains the bottle and rests it on a cleared portion of the table top. "That property's been overseen by three generations of my family. I don't like the whole notion of..."

His words are overpowered when noise and laughter erupt from the corner where Homer drags empty chairs across the cement floor to demonstrate a formation he thinks the high school team should employ.

"Put those chairs back where they belong, Homer," an irritated woman's voice scolds from behind the counter. "And leave those tables right where they are."

"Aw, Nell," he objects and continues sliding chairs into position, "nothing in your somewhat orderly arrangement will be disturbed more than a minute or two. If a customer comes in, I'll scoot everything back in place before you can holler in the order and collect the dollars."

The proprietress scowls but withholds comment when the front door slams behind a tall 40-something long-haired brunette who hurries to the counter.

"Let me have a big old glass of sweet tea, Nell," she requests.

"Connie!" Earline calls from across the room. "We're over here."

The brunette waves a hand in acknowledgment then exchanges two dollar bills for the tall glass that slides to a stop before her position at the counter. Her lips take a long pull on the straw before she confronts the jumble of chairs.

"Watch out there, Connie," sounds a male warning, "you're about to collide with a linebacker."

The brunette shifts the strap of her purse high on her shoulder, lifts her glass like the torch of the Statue of Liberty, and shouts "Homer Davenport! Who asked you to build an obstacle course in here?"

Nell's voice blares forth again, "He's about to be asked to *leave* if my chairs don't get put back where they belong."

"Oh, stop fussing," Homer fires back. "No harm's done, except disrupting what just might be the winning play our boys need."

Connie steps past him. "Winning play? Like the time you blocked the wrong way, let that Mount Pleasant defensive end nail Danny Clatterbuck, and we lost that nineteen eighty-eight playoff game?"

Loud hoots emanate from Homer's companions. He snorts and mutters while he shoves a chair hard against a table leg.

"Connie," Earline's voice soars above the din, "we're dying to know what you found out."

"I'm coming," Connie assures. She floats an air kiss peace offering to Homer and joins the two women at their table.

"Good news, ladies" she whispers. "We're in with the EMC." She keeps her voice low. "Not only will they let us use the auditorium without cost, but they will let us in first thing Veterans Day morning to set up and decorate."

"Wonderful!" exclaims Jo-Ella. "We sent the right woman, didn't we, Earline?"

"Kitchen access, too?" Earline asks.

Connie settles into a chair and speaks in a normal tone. "Of course. We furnish our own paper and plastic ware. OK to use the urns. We bring the coffee."

Earline scribbles on a yellow pad. "Jo-Ella?" she says but does not look up, "now you can advise Mister Berry... the Glee Club director at the high school."

That draws a fast "Consider it done."

"No slip-ups, Jo-Ella," Connie teases. "We don't want her filling more than one sheet on that pad."

"I know that's right," Jo-Ella concurs merrily.

Earline ignores them and continues making notes.. A shadow falls across her pad. She looks up as two men walk past on their way out.

"I'm not sure what you want me to tell them," a young man with a long paper tube in his hand is saying. He is a stranger to Earline, but the man with him bears a resemblance to someone she is certain she has seen before on local television or in newspaper photographs.

"We'll discuss it at the car," the older man advises the younger. They pass without speaking again and approach the odd maze of chairs. The younger man does not realize he has begun to walk alone.

"Good afternoon, Sergeant Davenport," the older man stops to address Homer, who is circling a chair, arms outstretched as if he expects a football will land in his hands.

Stunned, Homer grabs the chairback to halt without falling. "Why, Colonel Alsobrook! I never saw you come in. I sure hope our bit of fun didn't disturb...."

The older man extends his hand to the caught-in-the-act pseudo football coach.

"Not at all. This brings to mind some plays you orchestrated during off-duty hours in Desert Storm. Our reserve unit never suffered from boredom when you were around. Carry on... work out that pattern and have it ready should the Defense Department send reactivation orders."

"It would be a pleasure to serve with you again, Sir. Have a safe drive."

As Alsobrook steps past to follow the younger man to the parking lot, Homer's tablemates adopt a silent show of respect for the man they joked with mere minutes before.

Earline, too, has witnessed the scene. She whispers excitedly to Jo-Ella and Connie.

"Look what's just been dropped into our laps!"

Jo-Ella and Connie respond with blank stares.

"Our program needs a speaker. Who better than the man who commanded the Army Reserve unit from this area? He just walked past our table."

"Why didn't you stop him, Earline?" a wide-eyed Jo-Ella asks.

"Maybe we can catch him now," Connie urges.

"Here's a better idea," Earline whispers with a hand signal for low tones. "Let's get Homer to go out there with us!"

"Homer!" Connie calls sweetly, "can you take a time out from drawing up that play? We need you for a mission."

All three women rush at Homer, surround him, and begin a bombardment of pleas, explanations, and hints of favors to come if he'll join their cause.

'He looked awful busy," Homer protests.

"We won't interrupt," Earline promises. "When he finishes with that young gentleman, you can ask him."

"They may be traveling in the same car." he warns.

"All the more reason to get out there *now*!" Connie pushes against him. The four arms of Earline and Jo-Ella join with her two in propelling Homer toward the front door.

"What about my chairs?" Nell yells as the entourage hurries past her counter.

"They're old, they're uncomfortable, and they can't get much uglier while they wait til we get back," Connie snaps.

"I know that's right," chirps Jo-Ella.

5

The Parking Space

Just as Victoria was about to claim her prize, the nose of a black sport utility vehicle appeared suddenly to block the path of her silver sedan. Both drivers eyed the same open space in the mall's crowded parking lot, and neither appeared willing to yield an inch to the other.

With brakes engaged, each driver's stare intensified the standoff.

"This drizzly morning has been stressful enough already," Victoria muttered to herself. Her gums still hurt from repeated probes by the dentist's sharp instruments at a routine cleaning appointment. From that first stop, she went to place a bakery order only to be told it would take three days to fill. That meant she would have to return for the cake the very afternoon of her daughter's birthday party. Now this mall, where Victoria agreed to join a friend for lunch, presented an obstacle in the parking lot

She avoided a ramp to an upper deck and circled the sheltered ground-level lot without success until the second pass revealed a space had opened a short walk from the mall entrance. Now the standoff with a car that approached from the opposite direction at the same precise moment deepened her gloom.

The driver of the SUV seemed equally determined. And she had size on her side. The SUV and Victoria's Honda inched forward as if directed by some mad choreographer until each driver succeeded in preventing any possible entry by the other. Seconds ticked away. Each driver waited for her opposite number to give in.

Out of the corner of her eye Victoria became aware of movement beyond her side window. She dared not avert her gaze from the SUV, but the distraction demanded at least a slight share of her attention. A quick glance revealed a person standing beside her car. This person's upraised arms, shopping bags dangling from each hand, presented a sort of "I come in peace" gesture.

Victoria lowered her window halfway.

The distraction had a woman's voice.

"I've been trying to get your attention," the voice said. "My car is parked in the space beside the open one you want. If you'll back up, I'll be able to get out. Both cars can be accommodated."

Victoria smiled for the first time since she entered the bakery.

"Ma'am, I'm so grateful to you," she called to the helpful woman "May your good turn be rewarded in double measure." She shifted the Honda into reverse then, with a cavalierlike sweep of hand, motioned the contested space was the SUV driver's to claim, free and clear.

6

The House at the Corner
of Main and Cherry

Neal swept the business end of his broom across the tiled entrance to his art gallery and framing shop as a signal he would like to get back to work. His new neighbor did not take the hint; he wanted to talk.

"Why does the town tolerate that eyesore?" asked the young man who moments before introduced himself as the new manager of the furniture store next door to Neal's place of business. The man's ruddy complexion and shaved scalp flushed bright as the jeweled stud in his left earlobe. The object of his concern was a two-story Victorian-styled structure flanked by towering oak trees that remained an isolated testament to a former century.

"I don't believe many folks consider it an eye-sore," Neal defended the house on the opposite corner of Main and Cherry Streets. "That's the Detwiler-Graham house. Our town's simply grown up around it. It's the last of the handsome old houses that lined these streets leading in and out of courthouse square, the center of business a hundred years ago. The town grew... they built a new courthouse at a different location, but office buildings and retail shops such as ours began to crowd people who lived in those old houses so they moved farther out. Miss Hannah Graham's family stayed put."

The newly arrived furniture merchant stared in disapproval.

"She must be allergic to the smell of fresh paint." His sarcasm hung as heavily as dust and accumulated traffic residue that dulled the last coat of pine forest green applied to the house's wooden exterior. What once were cream-colored touches to lacelike trimwork at windows and the front veranda had faded to a grayish hue. Runaway ivy blanketed the grounds, centered by a wrought-iron fountain that had not bubbled in several years but still featured twin cherubs of marble facing each other at its top. A stone walkway circled the fountain on a path from the sidewalk to the veranda, free of the ivy except where two of four pilasters had been claimed by tentacles that threatened to reach the roof.

"Somebody should demand the town council do something," he groused.

The recent death of the former store manager brought this graduate of the statewide furniture chain's management program in Atlanta. He might know furniture, Neal reckoned, but the man would need time to come to an understanding of small town ways.

"Your predecessor knew Miss Hannah well," Neal said. "Her family's been prominent in this community in several ways, and I'm sure all that's very familiar to present members of the council. I expect some of 'em were once part of the parade of trick-or-treaters who scooped a handful of candy and gum from the basket Miss Hannah presented when they knocked at her door on Hallowe'en. She keeps that custom today."

The background summation did not impress the furniture man. His neck bulged atop the knot of a dark purple tie and tight white collar. The man's flushed face and glistening bald head prompted Neal's mischievous visualization of a big white onion with its outer layer peeled to expose an even shinier surface.

"You mean the whole town lets one old lady stand in the way of progress?" The man thrust his left arm toward the house in a gesture for emphasis. "Somebody ought..."

Neal's upraised hand silenced the man in midsentence. A taxi slowed to a stop at the curb in front of the house. "Maybe you shouldn't point," Neal said. "Here's Miss Hannah now."

They watched the driver get out and open the rear door to the passenger side where he extended an arm to assist a small, hatless woman with bobbed snow white hair in leaving his taxi. The two exchanged a few words before the woman mounted the single step up from the sidewalk. The driver stood and watched her walk cautiously with the aid of a cane through the ivy to the house. The absence of adornment of any kind with the pale blue dress she chose to wear suggested an unpretentious attitude toward whatever the woman's mission had been. The driver returned to his steering wheel, and the taxi moved on.

"We're going to be neighbors so I want to be on good terms," Neal resumed, "but I must ask that you lower your voice... and don't point like that. You'll discover sound travels well across the short distance when traffic slows. From time to time you'll overhear Miss Hannah's playing records by the singer Mario Lanza. The one she plays most often is 'The Loveliest Night of the Year.'"

Neal could see this news did not relieve the exasperation in the face confronting him but more needed to be said.

"Probably a legacy from her youth. Lanza was at the peak of his popularity in the nineteen fifties... when Miss Hannah was in her late teens and twenties.

There's a story of her love for a young man who was killed in the Korean War. A different version says he was a geologist who died in a mining accident. If she had other romances, the accounts aren't repeated like those two. The man who built the house, back in the eighteen-eighties, was Mister Arthur Detwiler, a cotton broker and financier...Miss Hannah's grandfather. His daughter, Miss Hannah's mother, is said to have been a sickly woman seldom seen. Her husband, Major Graham...Miss Hannah's father... was a decorated officer of World War One...well-groomed and authoritative. I remember him well. He looked after the Detwiler interests. Miss Hannah, their only child, now lives alone. You'll see her housekeeper come and go from time to time, and that woman's grandson sees to an occasional repair or errand. They deflect questions about the mistress of the house with silent smiles, so don't bother asking."

"I appreciate the history lesson," Neal's new neighbor interrupted. His agitation had not been calmed by the lengthy explanation. "That was yesterday. This is now. My firm has invested in providing a service to residents in this town... quality furnishings for their homes at reasonable prices without need to drive fifty miles to find similar quality and selection. In return, this town should maintain a clean, safe, inviting atmosphere where shoppers feel comfortable. Without some leftover relic of the past staring them in the face."

The strings of Neal's patience had been stretched near their break point.

"I've been in this location five years," his voice took a firmer tone, "and I've seen a steady flow of shoppers in and out of your company's store during that time. I don't recall the late Mister Nicholson ever saying the neighborhood had a negative effect on the store's sales volume. Do you mind telling me just what those folks in Atlanta said you should expect here?"

"Our management program prepares us to maximize the potential of our stores," came in rapid response. "We can't be limited by yesterday's methods. Our stores should be showplaces of style... compliments to the aura that buds in the mind of someone who desires to change the interior throughout a home. Our own exterior surroundings must not be a handicap to that thinking. In sum, we cannot allow our showplace to be dimmed by its neighborhood. Your storefront has a clean, inviting appearance. That throwback across the street does not."

Before he spoke, Neal studied the younger man's eyes, aflash with excitement and pride in the declaration.

"What you say makes sense... if your store is in a big shopping mall where appeal to the eye is critical and comparison is so easy. But you happen to be in a small town... where trust and service during and after the sale have great meaning. Evidently they did not explain that very well when they told you to come down here"

The new neighbor's eyes did not blink. "I believe I can be a force for change in merchandising here," he said with confidence. "And I'll begin by attending the next meeting of the town council to do what no one else seems willing to do... address the problem across the street and call for action."

"Before you go," Neal suggested, in a deliberately quiet tone, "perhaps you should take a look at your lease."

"All that's taken care of in Atlanta. I was shown a copy of our longterm arrangement with D and G Properties, headquartered there."

Neal did not try to hide his grin. "The headquarters may be there, but the major shareholder in D and G Properties is Miss Hannah Graham. Her father set it up before he passed. His nephew owns a minor share and handles all Miss Hannah's accounting, taxes, and such from his office in Atlanta. Be aware the house you'd like to remove is the home of your store's landlady."

The confident expression in the young man's face dissolved into bewilderment.

"And mine," Neal added in a gesture to lessen his new neighbor's embarrassment. "As well as a half dozen other stores in town."

7

Don't Look Down

Their self-directed tour of Scotland's Highlands brought them to Glenfinnan at Dan's insistence. His first reward came in Alicia's blissful "Oh, My...what a beautiful setting" as they walked toward the slender monument positioned alone and looming above the narrow end of the cradle that is framed by hillsides holding the waters of Loch Shiel.

"How tall is it?" Alicia asked. "I see people up there...alongside that statue on top."

A lad whose head barely cleared the parapet rail peered down at them while a second figure huddled beside him.

"Guidebook says sixty-five feet," Dan said. "That's about the same as a six or seven-story building. I think I'll climb up. Want to go with me?"

"No, you go ahead. Wave to me... I'll take your picture."

"Should give a terrific view of the loch," Dan called over his shoulder. He wondered if the late summer day was anything like the one in August 1745 that greeted the prince who landed on this shore of Loch Shiel to raise the standard of his father, the exiled King James VIII, and unite the clans in a mission to reclaim the throne of England, Scotland, Wales, and Ireland. For all descendants of Scots blood – and Dan claimed a drop or two – the Glenfinnan Monument stands for that bold if brief chapter of history. Good reason to pay homage, he suggested to Alicia when they planned each stop of their Highlands tour.

He entered a fortress-like stockade and crossed to the base of the column built of blocks of the same mottled grey stone. An open doorway led immediately to the first step of a circular stairway within the tower. Five steps up he yielded room so the boy – obviously no more than 10 years old – and a woman in back of him could descend.

A song ran through Dan's head as he climbed. "Wee bonnie boat, like a bird on the wing... over the sea to Skye. Carries the boy, born to be king... over the sea to Skye."

Wrong venue, Dan realized. Those lyrics were a better fit for the ill-fated prince's departure, not his arrival when optimism surged. He switched to sing

"Charlie is my darling, my darling, my darling... Charlie is my darling, the young Che-va-li-er." That ended as quickly as it had begun because Dan could not recall any more of the tribute to a hero of Scot legend and pride.

Round and round he ascended, each step calling to mind the spiral path of a bullet along the swirls of the bore inside a rifle barrel. Dan launched himself voluntarily, but he sensed another force at work in his upward trajectory.

Heritage. Adventure. Curiosity. Each played a part to motivate this climb. He had not expected they could, in combination, take control. He stumbled. Unchecked, momentum might propel him – like that bullet – into the sky. He slowed his pace deliberately when bright light descending upon him signaled the opening was near..

Two steps shy of the landing, he leaned forward to run his hand along the parapet's stone floor. The uneven, worn surface did not inspire a rush to stand. Heights had never bothered Dan. This strange setting, however, required determined effort to make the rest of his body obey and follow that arm. He crouched between the low wall and the base of the statue of a kilted Highlander permanently poised to go where his prince might command.

Dan gulped air. The parapet where he knelt did not appear more than eight feet in diameter. The base of the statue dominated the center. Through a gap in the wall that supported the iron railing he spotted Alicia, one hand shielding her eyes from the sun, gazing in expectation.

He braced his left arm against the statue's base. Next he moved cautiously from the crouch to a stoop then realized the level of his head at that moment was higher than the head of the boy who very likely stood erect to see across the railing. How easy it could be, Dan thought, to rise to his full six feet, three inch height and topple over that rail to his doom.

"So this is what acrophobia is like," he muttered as he knelt again.

He heard Alicia call from below. "Come on... stand up."

Dan tried summoning willpower to stand, but his state of near paralysis would not allow it.

"What's the matter?" Alicia again. "No one will believe it's a picture of you if you don't stand up," she scolded.

His shame rose although his body would not. How would he explain freezing to immobility atop a 65-foot stone column because it seemed a whole lot narrower at the top than it appeared from the ground? What if someone followed up the stairs to find him kneeling here? What could he say?

His panic, mounting with each breath, was penetrated suddenly by sound. A throaty hum. It exceeded the beating of his heart. The hum seemed to gain volume. Bagpipes? A ghostly echo of the clans? Filing down the hills to the sound of pipes on their way to join the prince in 1745?

No, this sound seemed to come from higher up.

Slowly, Dan forced his head back so that he could look upward past the statue. From his left, toward Fort William, he spotted a small propeller-driven plane flying northwest toward the isle of Skye. The little yellow-and-white plane glistened in morning sunshine.

Looking elsewhere besides the ground brought a calming effect, but Dan's panic returned once he realized the plane's occupants would see a grown man crouched in terror atop one of their popular landmarks.

"Can't let 'em see I'm chicken," he vowed. He grabbed hold of the iron rail with his right hand. Still resting his left against the statue's base, he took a deep breath, shifted his shoulders back, demanded that his legs supply thrust, and slowly achieved an erect if wobbly position. A few seconds pause to ensure balance brought the confidence needed to release his grip on the railing. He raised his right arm high and waved, first to the passing plane, next to Alicia.

"Finally," he heard her say.

"Zoom in for a close-up," Dan attempted to joke. He silently prayed his voice did not betray him.

8

Uncle Fox

The way the boy kept his head down when he entered the barn told Forest Larrabee something was not right. Within 15 minutes after the schoolbus dropped him off, ll-year-old Wade Larrabee could be counted on to join his great uncle at chores. He was his usual prompt self even this afternoon when he headed straight for the ladder to the hayloft without saying a word.

The agile boy sprinted up and down the ladder so effortlessly that upper part of the barn had become his personal territory. He snipped the thin metal strips binding hay bales stored there, tossed pitchfork loads to the floor below, then scrambled down to distribute shares of nourishment to livestock stalls.

This time he found Forest waiting at the foot of the ladder.

"Hold on," the big man said. He spotted a slick reddened lump beneath Wade's left eye. "How'd that happen?"

"Aw, it's just a bruise," the boy muttered, turning his head to escape close inspection.

"Let me see," the great uncle said and forced the boy to stand still.

"Mom's already looked it over, Uncle Fox. She smeared stuff on it. Got bumped by an elbow...in Phys Ed."

"Then why hide it from me? You're sure that mark wasn't left by somebody's knuckles?"

Embarrassed, the boy tried to move away. His captor held fast.

"Look here, Wade. If you've been in a fight, your mom will hear about it. Moms talk to other moms. And if you don't tell your side of what happened now, your dad will sure raise thunder when he gets home this weekend. Why don't you tell me? I might be able to help your mom accept what went on."

"I don't want to talk about it, Uncle Fox."

The form of address was a relic from Wade's infancy. When his parents taught him to say Uncle Forest in speaking to his father's uncle with whom they shared the Larrabee family farm and ranch, the child's best effort made Forest sound like Fox. The name stuck, and no one seemed to mind. The older man unashamedly demonstrated his feeling for the youngster who tagged along behind him at any opportunity. Their bond was not expressed in words but was evident to all who saw them together. Such a sighting would most likely occur on the Larrabee place because Forest left it on rare and brief occasions – to vote, visit a doctor, answer a summons for jury duty, or when persuaded by his nephew, Wade's father, to help transport livestock to or from a sale. He fulfilled a basic need of companionship through family conversation, turned daily to his Bible for inspiration, and consulted the newspaper for community, state, and national matters considered worthy of his interest.

Forest kept to home because it was the simplest way to avoid stares and whispers behind his disfigured body. At age 77 he wished only to do his part maintaining the Comanche County homestead established by his parents and return the love given him by the family of his late brother Wade, grandfather of 11-year-old Wade Larrabee. Forest bore no rancor when surprise showed in faces of strangers seeing him for the first time, however he grew tired years ago of retelling how his big, once powerful body had been misshaped into a hump-backed, perpetually bent form whose walk was a stagger. The fact his own lack of self control had contributed to the permanent condition made it even less pleasant to discuss.

The boy's "I don't want to talk about it" could not be misunderstood by a man who chose to adopt the same custom for his own reasons.

Forest's withdrawal into the protective cocoon of the farm and ranch suited that choice. His family respected his wishes and took care of what needed attention off the property. Schoolboy Wade, on the other hand, must go out into the wider world every day. If something in that exposure troubled him, the boy needed to confide in someone he trusted. In the absence of his father, who could listen better than the surrogate grandfather?

Forest relaxed his grip on the boy's shoulder. "Will you tell me what happened if I promise I'll listen and won't interrupt? Like the time you worried how to tell your dad you ran the tractor and harrow across his newly laid irrigation hose?"

Wade continued to avoid eye contact but stopped the struggle to move away.

"It's something I'll take care of," he said, barely above a whisper.

"Go on," Forest coaxed, "tell me the rest." The pause gave him time to examine the boy's face closely. The flesh was swollen along the cheekbone but did not yet promise a black eye.

"Just talk," Wade added.

"Talk you took exception to?"

The boy turned as if anxious to attend to the hay strewn on the barn floor. "Yes, but I'll take care of it."

"Sometimes talk leads to trouble. I guess it comes down to deciding if the talk is worth the trouble. Some talk can just be left to the wind... won't be missed when it's gone."

"It's worth it to me," Wade grunted.

"Well," Forest spoke slowly while he withdrew his hand. "I suppose you're the best judge of that. Just remember how water splashes and ripples when something big drops in the middle of a pond. Water spreads out in all directions... and sometimes the spills cause harm that's not expected. What gets settled...whether it's a big rock sinking to the bottom, or if somebody wins a fight... may cause a spillover. Other people... like your dad and mom... could get wet....."

"It's already 'bout family. I won't take it," Wade erupted.

The boy abandoned the attempt to hide his eyes. Forest studied them carefully. He had seen that same determined expression many times when Wade struggled to master a new skill.

"Take what?"

"Smart remarks...lies." He looked away again.

Forest returned his hand to Wade's shoulder, this time with affection. "Well, you know your dad and mom are as fine as anybody in this county... and the

Larrabee name has an honest reputation, so..." His voice trailed off but he did not release the shoulder hold. He forced the boy to face him.

"Something about me, was it?" he asked quietly.

Once Wade and his sister Emily boarded their schoolbus the following morning, Forest told Phyllis, the children's mother, he intended to request to speak to the boys in Wade's class and what it concerned.

"Ask them to include the girls," she advised. "Uncle Fox, you may not realize that girls can be just as bad as boys when it comes to taunting and bullying."

That surprised him, but he promised to heed her counsel.

He wedged his bulk behind the wheel of the farm pick-up truck and drove straight to the Audie Murphy Middle School parking lot. With classes in session, he remained unnoticed until he opened the outer door of the principal's office.

The secretary's astonished face neither surprised nor deterred him.

"I'm Forest Larrabee... may I speak with the principal?"

The woman's eyelids fluttered. The fingers of her right hand stroked her chin nervously until she regained sufficient composure to speak.

"She... has a full schedule." Awkward pause. "Does it concern one of our students?"

"I believe it does," Forest replied. "More than one, actually." From the way the woman leaned away from her desk, he gauged he may have spoken louder than intended. No matter, he decided, He had come seeking attention in the first place. That wish was answered when a woman stepped through the open doorway of an inner office in back of the secretary's position. She looked younger than the secretary although her self assurance encouraged Forest to relax.

"Are you the principal?" he asked in lowered voice..

"I am... Susan Gilchrist is my name. And I believe I overheard you say you are Mister Larrabee... is that right? How can we help you?"

"It's my appearance, Ma'am. If you're new to Comanche, you probably don't know that some folks are put off by the sight of me. I believe it's caused trouble among some of the boys in your school....sixth grade, particularly."

The young woman's eyes remained steadily fixed on his own while he talked. He did not see fear in them, and that encouraged his trust.

"Come into my office, Mister Larrabee," she invited. "Mrs Hoover, please see that we are not interrupted." With that, she motioned that Forest should precede her before she closed the door behind them.

Less than an hour later, the principal escorted Forest to an empty classroom where she invited him to be seated behind the teacher's desk. Ms Gilchrist waited just inside the hallway door. Soon a single file procession of sixth grade boys and girls wearing expressions of disinterest, puzzlement, or simple relief at being freed from class entered the room. Forest looked out the windows to avoid their glances and waited. Once Ms Gilchrist directed the students to be seated, she explained they were to return to class as soon as this session ended, introduced their guest, and went to sit at the back of the room.

Forest placed his palms on the desktop and rose behind it.

"I've been a subject of curiosity most of my long life," he began. The questioning eyes of more than three dozen youngsters did not boost his confidence, but the importance of his mission drove him to continue.

"I realized long ago that I'm not easy to look at. So I keep to myself as much as possible... hoping that will help folks go about their business without my presence making them uncomfortable. I've heard some of the jeers and ridiculous tales about me. They don't bother me much any more. But it cuts me to the bone when the talk hurts my family. Taunts like that bother me. You see it was a taunt that led to my being in the shape you see before you. That taunt just kept eating at me... relentless...and when I could stand it no longer, I made the mistake of my life."

He swallowed, paused to regain confidence, and stepped away from the desk. He presented his full left profile, and turned to provide a full-height view of the right. When the gasps subsided, he faced forward again.

"I wasn't born like this. I had a normal childhood, grew strong, stronger than other boys when we were about the same age you are now. By the time I reached my teens, I could outwork my daddy and most men around. Lifting livestock, sacks of feed and fertilizer, tossing bales of hay will do that for you when you do it every day. Before I turned sixteen I won a lifting contest at the county fair. That led to challenge after challenge over the next year. Sort of like the old gunfighter we've all heard about, always some pistol-happy cowboy itching to take him on. I thought I had to accept every lifting challenge that came. You see, that's what taunts can do."

When he paused for breath he became aware of the room's stillness and attentiveness in the eyes and ears waiting for him to continue. He did not possess an orator's skill, but he figured he'd best clear his throat quickly and finish his account or that attention would waver.

"Some neighbor boys kept after me to prove I could lift the front end of a car. The one they gathered round was a four-door Studebaker sedan. You probably don't know that car. They stopped making them before you all were born. I didn't doubt I could hoist the front end a foot or so off the ground if I backed up to it, bent my legs... you see, that way the legs do most of the work... and reached back beneath my knees to grip the front bumper. As soon as I took hold, three of them whipped doors open and jumped inside. I refused the bait and walked away.

"But that wasn't the end of it. They told anybody who'd listen how they had gotten the best of me... that I backed off, a champion disgraced. I should have ignored the talk... and I did where those boys were concerned, but it was harder to listen when grown men began to repeat it. I didn't like hearing my family's name trashed like that. It got so bad that, one day at the cotton gin, a man I didn't even know offered to bet anybody ten dollars that I couldn't hoist a five-hundred pound bale of cotton off the dock. Ten dollars was a lot of money in the nineteen-fifties. I didn't want to have a thing to do with it, nor did I want anybody of my family's acquaintance to feel a need to defend me. I yelled for the man to put his money away and said I'd lift the bale free of charge."

Forest took up a position with his back to the desk.

"I backed up to the dock like this, raised both arms above my head, and reached back to clasp the burlap webbing that encased the cotton bale."

His disability prevented full extension of his right arm, but he could tell by the hush in the room his listeners followed the demonstration with keen interest.

"Slowly… I pulled the bale forward onto my back, rested it there a few seconds, made sure of my balance, then stepped away from the dock. I heard those loud cheers and managed a few more steps before I turned back. When I moved to drop the bale to the dock, I stumbled and the weight shifted hard on my right side. My shoulder was crushed, a good bit of my upper back, too, before I got that bale back on the dock. Some men rushed me to the hospital and got word to my daddy. He sacrificed every dollar he could scrape up over the next year, took me to a big hospital in Fort Worth, but there was just too much damage to repair all of it. My lifting days were over, and I've looked like this ever since."

Forest returned to stand in back of the desk.

"Why did I come here to tell you all this today? Well, as I said a few minutes ago there's been some wild things said over the years. That I'm an alien left behind from that flying saucer some folks claimed they saw years ago in New Mexico. That I was kicked off a moving train and landed on the track… that I ran off to join the circus and got stepped on by an elephant… on and on. Truth is, I let someone's taunting and teasing push me to make a big mistake. I was a few years older than you are now, but you're not too young to learn from my mistake. Whenever someone taunts you, or dares you to do something, remember your own well-being is too important to risk trying to gain respect from someone who is not your friend anyway."

The silence that followed was broken by Ms. Gilchrist's voice from the back.

"Thank you for coming, Mister Larrabee. Boys and girls, file out now and return to your home room."

Forest slumped down in his chair. He watched the parade to the hallway and caught sight of Wade striding along, head held high, face beaming. That was reward enough, but an unexpected one came after the last child left the room.

"Texas has produced many brave men, Mister Larrabee," the principal said. "One of them honored my classroom with his presence today. Thank you for providing such a valuable lesson to young minds in my care."

Susan Gilchrist extended her slim hand. Forest rose to clasp it gently within his big callused fist.

9

G

A man halted work on the opened gate when the crunch of the rental Nissan Altima's tires announced an entry to the cemetery's gravel-covered driveway.

"Good morning," Alex called out from the steering wheel. "Can I give you a hand with that gate?"

"Thank you... no," the man answered. "Just takes awhile to loosen the screws on these hinges. Weather makes the heads crust over. You're not from around here, are you?"

"Good guess," Alex complimented. "I'm from out of state. I'd like to look for the graves of some of my mother's people. Do you take care of the cemetery?"

"Yes, I'm the caretaker. Town don't pay me much... but then I don't *do* much. Just unlock the gate in the morning and close it up at sundown. Ride the mower around every now and then. Bishop's my name."

Alex took him to be 70 or thereabouts, friendly in demeanor but curious for some identification in return. This small town in northwest Georgia should not be expected to differ from any other community of like size in the way one of its citizens would react to the appearance of a stranger.

"I'm Alex Saint John... pleased to meet you Mister Bishop. My mother's great grandfather was named McCall. We believe he was buried here... a little over a hundred years ago. Ever hear that name?"

Bishop pointed with his screwdriver toward a hill at the center of the cemetery. "There's a McCall tombstone back in the old section. I believe the rest of that family moved out west. I grew up in this county... never knew any McCalls myself."

"That's helpful. Does the driveway lead to the old section?" Alex asked.

"See that marble arch on that hill yonder? Well, you follow the driveway on around beyond it. You'll see a line of rosebushes on your left. Stop your car along there. That's the old section. Walk in back of the roses. I'd go along with you, if you wanted company that is, but right now I need to finish what I've started."

"Thank you... I'll have a look around," Alex said as he eased the car forward.

The driveway's gravel coating extended in a Y to the crest of the hill. Packed clay then formed the road surface atop the plateau. The tall archway appeared to center a part of the burial ground enclosed within a low wall made of rock that lined the left side of the driveway up the hill then crossed horizontally behind the arch and accompanied the opposite arm of the Y in its gravel-coated descent to the entrance. Alex drove past the wall's rightmost corner and along the top of the hill until he spotted rosebushes – in full bloom. He stopped the car, grabbed a clipboard, his camera, a roll of drafting paper, and set out to explore on foot.

He found what had been described as the old section filled that area outside the wall at the top of the Y and within the sweeping arc made by the driveway. Pioneer settlers were buried here, Alex reasoned, and very likely inside the walled enclosure, too. As the town grew, the large fan-shaped outer rim evidently had been opened to accommodate more recent burials where markers extended to a dense line of trees.

The caretaker kept the grounds presentable, but the old section included several tombstones that were broken, toppled, or sunken into the ground. Alex braced himself for a similar finding because his mother said none of her surviving McCall kin lived east of the Mississippi River, hardly within range to keep an eye on the condition of family memorials. To his relief, he saw McCall engraved on a granite stone, stained by weather and time, but standing erect on its base.

The stone marked the resting places of Samuel McCall, 1840-1903. and Jane, 1844-1902, great grandparents of Alex's mother. Samuel and Jane's son Grant McCall, grandfather of Alex's mother, led the migration to Oklahoma in 1910. Alex began a search for the grave of any of Grant McCall's three siblings. He found two markers close by with only the names Benjamin McCall and Latitia McCall legible. The figure of a lamb atop each stone suggested death in childhood. He photographed each tombstone then, for good measure, knelt to tape a sheet of soft paper to the face of the granite and brushed a stick of graphite across the inscription to make the letters appear on a rubbing he would take to his mother.

These tasks accomplished, he stood and scanned the ground for the third sibling's grave, Alex's mother's great aunt, in whose honor she had been given the name Genevieve. He was told this woman had been a favorite of Alex's grandmother, before the little girl left Georgia in 1910. She never saw Aunt Genevieve again, underscoring significance of the name she gave her own child, born in 1925.

Several stones near the McCall graves were overgrown with lichen. That forced Alex to kneel again and claw with his fingers to make even the surnames legible.

He crawled on his knees from marker to marker, scattering his equipment in the process, without finding anything that seemed relevant.

"Who are you looking for?" A woman's voice startled him.

Alex had seen no other person since he left the gate. He twisted his upper body into a half turn for a better view of his visitor. A woman stood facing him, but the morning sun beamed directly behind her. Half-blinded, he saw her in shadow.

"Hello....I didn't realize anyone else was here," he said. "I'm searching for the grave of Genevieve McCall... a great aunt of my mother."

"Did your mother go with her parents to the west?"

"No, *her* mother did." Alex wiped the back of his hand across his eyes and tried to overcome the sight advantage his visitor held. "*My* mother was born in Oklahoma... fifteen years after the family moved. Mother was named for Genevieve."

"Genevieve's not buried here," the woman said.

"Do you know where?" Alex asked. He started to get to his feet, but the flapping of one of the paper rubbings distracted him. The tape had failed to hold. A slight wind threatened to carry the tissue-thin paper away.

He heard the woman say "You need to go to the Hunter family's graves... Raleigh." as he scrambled after the elusive sheet of paper.

"Can you tell me where that is?" he called over his shoulder. He snatched the paper from its lodging against a tombstone and looked back.

His visitor had disappeared.

He rolled the paper against his thigh to form a tube. The distraction cost him an opportunity to gain important information. With no idea where the Hunters were buried, he had no choice other than a return to ask the caretaker at the entrance.

The sound of Alex's tires on the gravel alerted Mr. Bishop. He lifted the screwdriver in greeting.

"Did you find the McCalls?" he asked.

"Some of them. A woman came up while I knelt to copy dates and such." Alex flipped the gearshift to park and stepped out of the car. "She said I needed to go to the Hunter section to find the grave of one of the McCalls, but she left so suddenly I didn't get to ask where the Hunter section is.... even if it's in this cemetery. Did she pass you on her way out?"

The caretaker frowned. "No one's been here all morning... except you."

"But I talked to her," Alex insisted. "Do people walk in from another entrance?"

"Ain't no other entrance," Bishop declared. "Fence goes all around the cemetery. The Boatwrights... and the Tibbles, too, live back beyond the treeline. But both women are about as old as me. No chance they'd climb over that fence. What did this woman look like?"

"Well, I didn't see her plain because she stood between the sun and me. Looking into that bright sunshine, I couldn't tell much about her. Sort of a silhouette, you know? Long hair, loose-fitting dress. Her voice didn't sound like that of an older woman."

Bishop may have been too polite to say he doubted what Alex described, but his eyes expressed it.

"Well, what about this Hunter section?" Alex asked. "Is that another graveyard? Or is it part of this one?"

The question brought a laughing response. "Oh, it's here, all right. Fact is, you were right next to it. The Hunters were well to do. Bartholomew Hunter just about founded this town singlehanded. He built the cotton mill ten years after the war... town grew up around it. That marble arch on the hill stands at the head of his grave. Nobody's buried inside the walls that surround it except Hunters....or some close kin of a Hunter.. You can go in and look around if you want. I take the mower inside through that ivy-covered arbor yonder," The screwdriver doubled as a pointer again,. "But you're tall enough to step over that low wall most anyplace you choose. Take care you don't step on the toes of that woman you said you talked to."

Alex chose to let Bishop enjoy his moment of humor, mumbled his thanks, and turned the car around to drive back into the cemetery. Then he remembered.

"You said Bartholomew Hunter, didn't you?" he called through the open window at the passenger side.

"Yes," Bishop nodded.

"Was there a Raleigh... or a Riley Hunter?"

"Raleigh was the son who was killed in the Spanish-American War. A good-sized marker... close by the old man's."

"Thanks again," Alex called. His foot pressed the accelerator. He drove back up the hill and stopped at the spot where he parked earlier. He decided to explore without the burden of equipment since he had no idea what he'd find, and it would take no great effort to return for camera, clipboard, or anything else. He walked in back of the rosebushes again and approached the Hunter wall from the crest of the hill. The rock wall looked about three feet high; no handicap to Alex's long legs. He stretched his right leg high, took a seat atop the wall for a second, then swung his left leg across and to the ground.

He headed straight for the arch. The white marble monument stood at least a foot higher than Alex's own six-foot height. The twin-columned supports were anchored on a wide base on which the name Hunter was carved across the downhill side. Beneath the surname, the name Bartholomew was inscribed, above the dates 1837-1916, opposite the name Phoebe, with 1848-1920 below.

Bartholomew and Phoebe had the entire row that crowned the slope to themselves.

Alex estimated about two dozen tombstones were within the entire enclosure. A good sized marker for Raleigh Hunter should not be difficult to find, he figured. It proved true immediately.

On the first level downhill from Bartholomew – below his right foot, one might say – stood a sturdy gravestone bearing the name Raleigh Hunter, beloved son of Bartholomew and Phoebe. The next line read March 7, 1875 – July 1, 1898. Carved beneath those dates were the words 1st Lt, U.S. Army, and below that, A Hero at San Juan Hill.

A fitting memorial, Alex thought, and all very informative. But what did it have to do with Genevieve McCall?

Several feet to the left of Raleigh Hunter's grave, along the same level, was a large tombstone identified Cochran. The given names were those of Anna H. Cochran and the man Alex presumed was her husband. A good distance from Raleigh's right side stood the marker of Jacob F. Hunter, and farther along, a tombstone for Stephen M. Hunter. A quick inspection of each inscription convinced Alex this row was made up of graves of Raleigh Hunter and his siblings. The Hunter name, and that of Cochran, appeared frequently on graves in lower levels. Alex took them to be successive generations of Hunter descendants.

He walked back uphill and examined Raleigh Hunter's tombstone again. He ran his fingers up and down each side. Finding no mark other than those noted at first sighting, he stood for a moment at the foot of the grave. He had been blessed with good weather for graveyard inspection, and his search had met with some success. However, with the heat of the noonday sun bearing down, he felt dissatisfied because of that he failed to find.

He studied the position of Raleigh Hunter's burial spot in relation to the graves of his siblings He began to pace again, first several feet to his left, then an equal distance to his right. Any notion he might spot a flat stone marker in the act was dismissed after he retraced his steps twice. One thing did become more apparent. Raleigh's grave seemed closer to the Cochran marker of his sister Anna, at the soldier's left, than to his brother Jacob, at his right. But what did open space signify? And was it relevant to Genevieve?

Thirst became a problem. He decided to return to the car for his water bottle. He began to walk uphill between the graves of Jacob and Raleigh, stopped abruptly, and stared at the spot where his right foot had landed.

Virtually concealed by grass that had not been mowed recently, a flat, square plate of dark metal had been set into the ground. It appeared to be about six inches square. Alex bent to pull away some of the grass and brush the surface free of dirt. Dents along each side of the scarred plate suggested losing encounters with a lawnmower. The housekeeping by his fingers revealed the letter G etched in script. Nothing more. He gripped the sides of the flat object and tugged hard. Whatever anchored that metal plate had been driven deep into the ground.

"Could this be the grave of Genevieve McCall?" he whispered to himself.

After he drained the water bottle, Alex drove back for a third chat with the caretaker. The man needed to hear very few words before his head nodded in recognition.

"I know what you're talking about," Bishop interjected. "I've run over that thing...why I couldn't begin to tell you how many times. I figure it must have something to do with Raleigh's death in that battle. Nobody's ever told me any different."

"Does any of the Hunter family still live in town? Or close by?"

"Yes, but I doubt these younger ones would know much about something that's been there... I don't know how long... a hundred years or more."

The discovery recharged Alex's energy, and he was not about to quit the chase. "I'd sure like to talk with some of them."

Bishop placed both his hands atop the gate and stared toward the road. "Tell you what," he offered, "one of Anna Cochran's daughters is still alive. She's in a nursing home up at Rome. Don't know her situation at present... but last I heard, her mind was still sound. Stop in at the bank and ask to speak to Vickie Sanders... she was a Cochran before she married, She could likely tell you something about Mrs. Lily."

A little more than an hour later, Alex entered the lobby of Autumn Shades Nursing Home bearing a small vase of fresh peppermint carnations purchased at a Kroger store spotted on his drive into Rome. The clipboard tucked beneath an arm was the only item of equipment brought along.

He explained his mission to the woman at the front desk and sat down in one of several vinyl-covered guest chairs to contemplate the lives of tiny fish who populated an aquarium in the corner closest to him. He expected to wait awhile but was surprised to learn that would not be necessary. The object of his quest was in no mood for an early afternoon nap. She had issued orders that a man bearing flowers be brought to her side immediately.

A staff nurse escorted Alex to a small private room. Propped high with pillows at her back, 94-year-old Lily Cochran Scott looked him up and down then beckoned him to take the straight chair at her bedside. She reached for the flowers, gave them a good sniff, and returned the vase to Alex.

"They're lovely. Thank you, young man. Please rest them on that small table behind you so I can admire them all day long." A lilac-colored bed jacket embraced her shoulders, an enhancement for her blue eyes and pink complexion.

Alex apologized for his rumpled apparel and introduced himself as succinctly as possible. The names St John and McCall set Mrs. Scott to reminiscing about a St John who once wrote for the Atlanta newspaper and McCalls mentioned at various times in her life, but none of them made it into her circle of acquaintances.

When she paused, Alex explained his visit to the cemetery kept the promise made to his mother before he left Oklahoma City on a business trip to Atlanta. "You see, Mrs. Scott, my mother was born in 1925, a good many years after her folks settled in Oklahoma. She has never been to Georgia, but she recently expressed a desire to know more about the great aunt for whom she was named. I hoped to find... at the very least...where that woman is buried and take my mother a photograph..."

"What is your mother's name?"

"Genevieve. She was told by *her* mother that she... that is *her* mother... chose that name in honor of a favorite aunt, who she knew only when a small child before the family moved west." He repeated "My mother's mother's favorite aunt" for clarification.

"Are you talking about Genevieve McCall?"

"Yes, I did not find her tombstone in the same area where her parents and two little siblings are buried...."

"No, you wouldn't," Mrs. Scott interrupted. "She's not there." The lady rested her head against her pillow but kept her eyes on Alex. She studied him even more closely than the first appraisal when he entered the room.

He waited for this valuable source to take the conversation where she wished.

"Of course I can only tell you what Mama confided to me. Mama said Genevieve and Uncle Raleigh were sweethearts before he went into the army. He asked her to wait for him... because the war broke out so quickly and there was a hurry to organize... train the troops and so on. Uncle Raleigh was such a bright young man they made him an officer right away. He had just two days leave before they shipped off for Cuba. Of course that was the last time the family... or Genevieve... saw him. Mama kept a picture of him on her dresser. Handsome... Oh, I tell you my Uncle Raleigh was handsome."

Mrs. Scott closed her eyes. A long minute passed with the only sounds coming from the hallway. Alex dreaded to think she might fall asleep. His patience was rewarded. The eyes reopened and the narrative continued.

"The family was told, when Uncle Raleigh fell wounded, he was taken to what was called a field hospital. That's where he died... the same day. They say my Grandfather Hunter was a powerful man. He knew how to get something done and who ought to be able to do it. That's how the body was brought back. It took a while, I understand, but he got it done."

Alex kept quiet although he wanted Genevieve reintroduced in the account as quickly as possible. He did not have long to wait.

"I was told Grandfather chose that hillside for the family's graveyard some time before Uncle Raleigh was killed. I'm sure he thought the first ones buried would be Grandmother and himself. Mama said he personally marked off how the rest were to be placed around Uncle Raleigh's grave since he was the first one taken."

An even longer pause came next. Alex cleared his throat and shifted in his chair.

"I don't know if I should tell you this," Lily Cochran Scott began in a softer tone, "but you're the first of Genevieve's family I've ever met. I'd never say it to anyone else. I suppose you have a right to know."

Alex leaned closer.

"Mama said Genevieve just went to pieces when Raleigh got killed. Any young girl would have, I reckon, in the same circumstances. She taught school while they were courting, but when she learned he'd been killed she shut herself up at her parents' home...

just consumed by grief. The school had to replace her, of course. Mama said Genevieve came to Grandfather Hunter... first time anyone had seen her leave her house. She asked to be buried at Raleigh's side... vowed she'd never love anyone else. Grandfather refused. Mama said he never tried to hide that Raleigh was his pride and joy. No way he would dishonor his memory... why, if a woman who was not Raleigh's wife was buried at his side, folks would believe they'd carried on without shame."

A nurse entered, asking whether Mrs.. Scott needed anything. Alex dreaded any suggestion that his visit be cut short. Please, just a little while longer, he appealed silently to higher powers. He scribbled notes on his clipboard.

Lily Cochran Scott accepted the offer of a sip of water to freshen her throat then dismissed the nurse with a wave of hand.

"So Mister Hunter turned her down?" Alex asked in a gentle nudge to the spot where the story left off.

"That's what Mama said. Later on Genevieve had her father talk to Grandfather. Mama said Mister McCall offered to do anything he could in return, but that didn't change Grandfather's mind. A few years went by, her parents died, and Genevieve came up here... to Rome... to be a family's governess. That didn't last long. When she learned Uncle Jacob's wife was ill, Genevieve hurried back home and volunteered to see to their children. Aunt Mary was never strong after that, so Genevieve stayed on as housekeeper and governess. Mama said it was plain she did it to be close to Raleigh. And to her brother Grant's little girl."

"That little girl would have been Nora," Alex chipped in. "My grandmother."

Mrs. Scott smiled. "Well, you already know that Grant McCall moved his family out west. Genevieve would not go with them, even though her parents had passed before then. The love of her life had been taken, but she would not leave... not even to see that little girl grow up. Mama said it was so sad, but so beautiful, too. Such devotion."

The remembrance was soon displaced by one darker. "That awful tuberculosis began to spread about that time," Lily continued. "Mama said everybody was terrified because so little could be done for victims. That was before I was born. My cousin Maggie, Uncle Jacob's daughter, came home sick from school. Genevieve must have caught it while tending to her. She worked night and day caring for Maggie but made it worse for herself. By the time others could convince her that Maggie would recover, Genevieve was so weak she lived but a few weeks more."

Lily pulled a tissue from a box on a tray that overhung the right side of her bed. She dried her eyes and grew quiet.

Alex maintained a respectful silence before he spoke. "My mother said someone wrote to the family in Oklahoma that Genevieve died in 1913." He paused to ensure eye contact had been restored. "At the cemetery, I saw a metal plate with the initial G on it..."

"Then you are a lot more observant than most people," Lily said.

"Does it mean Genevieve's wish was granted? That she's buried there, at Raleigh's side?"

"Mama said it took some doing to make it happen, but she and her brothers insisted. Grandfather finally gave in. He had conditions, however. She could not be placed at Uncle Raleigh's left... where a wife would have been. That's why she's on his right side. Uncle Jacob suggested widening the space where his own grave was to go. Grandfather forbade any tombstone. He arranged the funeral himself... kept the mention in the newspaper at a brief line or two without any burial details. The metal plate with the single initial was his own idea. A concession he wasn't happy about, but it kept peace in the family."

"So Genevieve got what mattered most. To be buried beside Raleigh." Repeating the words aloud made Alex realize how surprisingly intense his search for confirmation had become.

Lily Cochran Scott smiled along with him. "Yes... Mama said even Grandfather seemed to finally accept that Raleigh must have loved the girl who remained so devoted to him alone. It's unfortunate your family didn't know more about it. Afterward it just wasn't talked about within Mama's family. She told me a lot more, I'm sure, than my uncles ever told their children."

"Well," Alex said as he got to his feet, "I'm so very grateful to you, Mrs. Scott, for sharing all you've told me. I know my mother will be grateful, too, when I confide so many things she never knew about the first Genevieve."

"Please give my regards to her," Lily said. "And thank you for coming to see me. I've often thought someone should have written a book about Raleigh and Genevieve. Their years were short, but their love was *so* strong. Mama witnessed it... and you've helped me call back memories of things she said to me. Bless you."

With another round of thanks, Alex left her and hurried to his car. If he stepped on it, he could get back to the cemetery before the gate closed at sundown. He needed to make one stop on the way to purchase a spray of fresh flowers. The long overdue time had come for some member of his family to place flowers at the grave of Genevieve McCall.

In the visit with Lily Cochran Scott he left untold his own experience with the spectral being who played such a key role in his search for Genevieve's grave. He had yet to decide what to make of it himself. Should the figure return, the flowers would confirm her advice had been followed. If she did not enjoy that satisfaction already.

Alex felt confident another rubbing and one more photograph – flowers in the foreground with Raleigh Hunter's tombstone in the background – would mean almost as much to his mother.

10

Two Tethers

The serpentine formation moves without harmony. This line's human participants share a common objective but have no leader.

Some face forward, eyes fixed on the back of the person in front. Others turn left or right to converse with a companion or total stranger between waist-high strips of fabric strung along each side that keep the line narrow. A few like Joe Kilpatrick are engrossed in displays on hand-held electronic devices or folded newspapers.

Their immediate destination is an airport security checkpoint where clearance will permit them to scatter to gates for departing flights that will carry them to cities where business or leisure await.

The routine is familiarly boring to frequent travelers like Joe. Rare is the week when a sales representative whose region reaches from Virginia to Colorado is not on an airplane. A veteran commuter fights the boredom that descends like a net when complying with precautions necessary for safe travel and seeks to turn time to advantage.

"Morning, Jeannie," Joe whispers to the phone in his hand. "Will you see that the Hastings survey we reviewed yesterday is faxed to Tess Philipson this morning? You'll find her number... Oh...you've done it? Did you ask Jeff whether... You did? Excellent... Thanks. I'm to meet with Tess at three this afternoon. Talk to you later."

Shuffling feet signal movement in front of him. Joe kicks his carry-on bag to close the gap left where those ahead have inched forward. He tries another number then breaks the connection once he realizes he calls into a time zone where no one will be at work for another hour. He shrugs and tucks the phone inside a side pocket of his luggage.

Forward in line, Joe sees a young woman tighten her grip on an orange fabric tether affixed to the backpack of a small boy. The boy, who appears to be about four, has strayed beneath the fabric strip. He is in the path of grown-ups going the opposite way. A gentle tug from the woman Joe presumes is the child's mother brings a quick return at her side. Some people who do not travel with a curious child might question her use of the restraint. Nor Joe. Good travel foresight, he admits, recalling his own precocious Tim when about this boy's age.

A different sort of tether hypnotically holds Joe and strangers ahead and behind him in a human chain whose links move cog-like if and when authority directs.

"Keep moving, please," the voice of a security worker rises above the mumbles and nervous giggles which prove this tether is composed of living if somewhat distracted persons. More than one face reveals apprehension and a few hands check pockets or make last-minute adjustments to items that will be presented for inspection. Joe has experienced this drill so often he forgets the fear that haunts an infrequent traveler who dreads being publicly singled out for some infraction of security rules.

Still he, too, grunts in irritation when some hold-up causes the snake-like line to halt. He checks his watch and calculates the minutes remaining before his plane is to depart. When he nears the steel-topped tables where plastic tubs await deposit of keys, coins, belts, purses, shoes, et cetera to accompany carry-on bags along the belt for X-ray examination, Joe stretches an arm and grabs two empty tubs. He offers one to the person in front of him in a hurry-along gesture then dumps his own personal effects into the second.

A chorus of sighs breaks out when the line halts again. Security personnel ask one traveler to step through the screening doorway a second time. They direct the man to another inspection station before a signal is given the rest to move forward again.

Once his turn comes, Joe passes through the full-body detection device quickly, retrieves his carry-on from the moving belt, begins a hasty transfer of small effects from the plastic tub to his person, and slips his feet into security-cleared dress loafers. He strides into a familiar hallway, turns left, and begins the short walk to his designated gate. Head spinning in a countdown of matters he will attend to once his flight is airborne, he arrives to find boarding already underway.

Joe surrenders his boarding pass and enters the sleeve-like enclosure to the door of the plane. The woman and boy he noticed earlier are ahead in line for the same flight. He admires the young woman's deft management of a carry-on bag with one hand while the other pulls back on the orange strap to slow the boy's attempted run down the sloped tunnel.

Passengers suddenly bunch up near the plane's open doorway. A prompt for Joe's sigh of recognition that someone already on board has found difficulty storing a bag in an overhead bin and now clogs the aisle.

Again he catches sight of the young woman. Her loosened grip on the orange tether has allowed her small charge to creep close to the aircraft he waits to enter. Through a narrow aperture formed where the wall of the boarding sleeve stops inches short of the passenger compartment a plane window is visible. The boy, on tiptoe, peeps through the open space for a glimpse inside that window then flashes an eager grin of expectation for the adventure that awaits him on board.. He responds to another gentle pull on his backpack, turns, jumps, and lands flat-footed upon the plane's carpeted threshold.

Joe laughs out loud in empathy with the excited boy. Precautions and tethers notwithstanding, flying can still be fun.

11

One Dilemma at a Time, Please

Room 116: one more door to open, one more dimly lit room to enter, one more blackboard on which Dahlia will erase the overnight nurse's name and replace it with her own while dawn ushers a new day for staff and patients of the big hospital.

Dahlia writes in bold strokes. Her cursive lettering emphasizes the D, the h, and the l with flourish befitting the colorful flower for which she was named 55 years ago this coming September. There is nothing timid about her oversized script. It conveys commitment. Those who see it will recognize an experienced nurse has reported for duty. Some shrewd observer may see in it a cry for help. That would not disappoint Dahlia. She feels distress but will not allow it to interfere with her work.

From the bed immediately in back of her, she overhears a sigh of satisfaction from Mr. Baldwin.

Dahlia turns to greet him. "So you like it when I have to go to work?" she teases.

"I rejoice when it's your name I see written on that board, Dahlia," the man answers from his pillow. "It tells me I'll have a friend in my struggle to get a few bites of breakfast down when a doctor pops in at the same time to check my incision or blood pressure... or someone comes with a needle seeking more blood. The other nurses ignore me when I ask for a hot cup of coffee to start over once I'm free of straps and needles. You understand, Dahlia. I appreciate that."

"Yes, I understand, Mister Baldwin," she assures. "That coffee gets cold mighty quick when you've been interrupted." Her good nature hides the fact her own breakfast had to be cut short in a rush to catch her bus because her little 10-month-old great grandbaby cried incessantly before Dahlia took time to massage the child's gums as comfort for teething. The baby's mother, Dahlia's 17-year-old granddaughter, hid her head beneath her pillow and pretended to sleep through it all. The task of providing for them had fallen to Dahlia six months ago when her own daughter, the granddaughter's mother, died from a drug overdose.

Dahlia has serious reason to trim her weight, but breakfast is her most substantial meal of the day. She needs that boost of energy to do her job.

Thirty-three years of nursing, the last eight at this hospital, have prepared Dahlia to cope. She must draw on that experience frequently to deal with crises within her own family. And pressure from the hospital's new head of nursing about appearance has placed one more heavy concern on her shoulders. Without open complaint, of course, since Dahlia stoutly believes her patients do not need to hear about her troubles. Her mission is to see them get well. But the way slim, little Miss Lori Hutchinson says the word 'obese' causes self-conscious Dahlia to consider herself a truck in a lot filled with compact cars.

"I see you're to be moved to Rehabilitation today," she looks up from examining the chart suspended from the frame at the foot of Mr. Baldwin's bed. "You're healing nicely from that hip replacement"

"Well, I know I'm going to miss you, Dahlia, when those therapists push....and push some more. Their agenda may not allow an old man much leeway."

"They'll treat you right, Mister Baldwin. You'll be home walking with a cane in no time," she encourages and crosses to open curtains drawn at the window. The rhythm in her movement exceeds that of snores sounding from the bed of the other patient in the room. Mr. Alvarez slumbers on this morning in whatever land his dreams have transported him. Unlike Mr. Baldwin, Mr. Alvarez is to remain where he is until those in charge determine his infected foot and overall diabetic condition are controlled sufficiently for transfer to a nursing home.

Dahlia decides to let him sleep when the sudden pulsing of her wrist monitor summons her to the hallway.

"Got to hurry, Mister Baldwin," she calls on her way to the door. "They should bring your breakfast tray in a few minutes. I'll check on you in a little while, OK?"

She hears Baldwin's assent as she closes the door behind her. A quick look left, then right, in the hallway where a light above the door tells her attention is needed in room 112. She hurries as fast as legs and feet move her 200 pounds safely past room 114 and a linen cart someone left in the hallway to reach and open the door of 112. The nightgowned body of Mrs. Finley lies crumpled beside the foot of the bed nearest the door. From a sitting position in the bed by the window, Miss Edenfield continues to press the call button.

"All right, Miss Edenfield," Dahlia soothes, "I'm here. You don't have to press that any more." With great effort, she kneels to determine if Mrs. Finley is conscious. The woman's silence suggests her head may have hit the floor when she fell. "Did you see what happened, Miss Edenfield?"

"Not at first," the frightened woman manages to reply. "I heard a little moan just as I saw her body go down. She could have been sitting on the side of her bed, for all I know. That thump scared me."

Mrs. Finley's position has the left side of her face flat against the floor. Dahlia strokes the head gently and bends close to whisper. "Mrs. Finley? It's Dahlia, honey. Do you hear?"

A soft release of breath escapes the woman's lips.

"Do you think you can get up if I help you, Mrs. Finley? This old floor's mighty hard... yes it is." Dahlia's own knees ache in a warning she might never stand again if she does not hurry to get up.

"Dahlia's right here with you, Mrs. Finley," she pledges above her own discomfort. She presses her wrist monitor to summon the technician for assistance.

Mumbled words sound from the woman on the floor. "Praise the Lord Jesus Christ," Dahlia whispers. "Don't leave me now, please Lord.. let me help this poor lady... and please help me get back up."

"Does it hurt along here?" she speaks at full volume, "or here?" as she runs a hand behind the woman's neck, underneath her shoulders, and along each limb.

A faint grunt from the floor is superseded by arrival of the technician who sees to equipment and furnishings in each room. Dahlia recognizes Nico, a husky young man who joined the staff two weeks before.

"Get the body board please, Nico. I don't think she's broken anything. We need to slide her onto the board then lift her safely back to bed. Please hurry."

The technician rushes to the hallway and returns a minute later, a full-length body board balanced across one shoulder. Dahlia struggles to make room between her own knees and the body of Mrs. Finley. "I'll slide her shoulders, Nico. Come around behind me and move her lower half."

They accomplish that first act as a team to the sound of mutterings from Mrs. Finley, then Dahlia signals the technician she needs aid herself. "Whew!... let me have a minute, Nico, before I try to stand," she begs once his supporting arm arrives at her elbow.

"What's happening?" a voice intrudes from the open doorway. A quick glance confirms it belongs to Mila, the nurse responsible for rooms on the opposite side of the hallway.

"It's all right, Mila," Dahlia says. "One of my patients tried to do too much on her own. We have it under control."

"Why didn't you turn the signal light off? And the room light on?" the Middle European-born Mila questions while she flips a switch by the door and moves to stand in back of Dahlia. "From here it's hard to tell who needs help first... the patient, or you."

Dahlia swallows her pride and chooses to make no reply until, with Nico supporting one arm and her grasping the frame of Mrs. Finley's bed with the other, she stands again. She turns to address Mila. "We'll manage. No need to keep you from your own patients."

The eyes of the other nurse appraise Dahlia, their judgment unhidden and unhurried. The silent, from toes up, scrutiny does not end until Dahlia, uncomfortable that her body would be assessed by a co-worker as well as the new director of nursing, returns her attention to Mrs. Finley and Mila has left the room.

Mercifully, Nico's voice stirs Dahlia's concentration from self-consciousness to the matter at hand.

"Change with me," he instructs. She welcomes the suggestion that he replace her at lifting the heavier torso and shoulders. In moving Mrs. Finley from the board to her bed, they manage to turn her body gently but not without more mutterings from the one who now lies on her back.

"Thank you, Nico," Dahlia sighs in gratitude. "I think we'd better raise the safety bars higher this time," she adds quietly. "While you do that, I'll see if she will tell me what was so important that she had to get up and tend to it by herself. Will you tell me, Mrs. Finley?"

"I want... to go...home," whispers the woman who has been returned to her bed.

"There, there," Dahlia comforts, "of course you do. But the doctors want you to stay here with us a little longer." She gently massages the woman's neck and shoulders while the technician raises and locks security barriers at each side of the bed's frame.

Once she is convinced her patient is unhurt and calm is restored to Room 112, Dahlia's morning routine has fallen 15 minutes behind schedule. She hurries to complete wake up rounds and dispense each patient's assigned allotment of medications, but the food service staff arrives, and she must apologize to patient and food server alike for being in the way. Crowd conditions at bedside remind her of Mr. Baldwin's lament. As soon as the last of her 12 patients downs his medication before her eyes, she looks in again at room 116.

"Does your cup need a refill, Mister Baldwin?"

Baldwin nods to show his pleasure in being remembered, his fork having filled his mouth with a generous serving of pancakes. Dahlia retreats to the end of the hallway, where a coffee urn is positioned on a supply counter beneath medicine lockers. A man and a woman stand in conversation before the long counter, their backs turned to her approach. When under some mutual agreement they decide to move on to another location, the woman turns first. Dahlia is face to face with Lori Hutchinson, Director of Nursing.

With a slight acknowledgment of recognition, the director pauses. "If I may have a moment, Doctor?" she asks her companion before she addresses Dahlia. "I'm glad you happened by. Please come to my office a few minutes after one o'clock. We'll talk further then."

Lori Hutchinson moves swiftly to keep the doctor from waiting, but the hasty call does not sit well on Dahlia's nerves. It is an unpleasant reminder how conspicuous she felt while enduring Mila's inspection.

She forces herself to return with a fresh cup of coffee for Mr. Baldwin, but the remaining hours of Dahlia's morning pass in a jumble of disconnected events, each one overshadowed by concern for what has brought this summons to the director's private office. She is sure it will be another lecture about losing weight. A third, and likely more intense session than the second, which was considerably more personal and stressful than the first meeting when obesity was singled out in a discussion of the hospital's recently revised 'protocol,' a word whose meaning Dahlia guesses includes grounds for dismissal.

"I admit I'm heavy, but my work gets done," she mumbles in self-consolation. "It's not that I haven't tried to lose weight. Lord knows, I try. Didn't I lose twenty-seven pounds already? Mama was a big woman, and I believe it's just natural that I inherited some of it from her. Nobody... I mean *no-body* can say I sit around like some lazy person. I've worked all my life.

"I've got to work," the self analysis continues. "Here I am... raising two new generations of children... at this time in my life! They have to be fed and clothed. And who'll keep them from sleeping on the streets if I don't? I wish somebody could answer that. I pray over it every night, and I talk with Preacher Ellison at every opportunity. 'Hold on,' he guides me, 'Keep holding on. Our Lord hears your prayers.'"

Each minute spent in meditation adds to her stress. She keeps to herself during the break for lunch. Her diet allows a microwaved cup of beef broth and a granola bar only. She seeks a corner of the break room to escape tempting aromas from the big table where others gather. Mila is not among them. Her absence feeds Dahlia's wonder if the summons to Miss Hutchinson's office has something to do with the early morning incident in 112.

When one o'clock registers on the big clock in the break room, Dahlia leaves for a careful re-examination of her appearance in the restroom mirror before she begins a cursory check in each of the six rooms of her charge. She spots a gurney exiting room 116, Mr. Baldwin's transport to the basement tunnel and the hospital's Rehabilitation wing. She hurries to clasp one of his hands.

"One more stop on your road to home, Mister Baldwin," she squeezes the hand in encouragement.

"I'll miss you, Dahlia," he calls as orderlies roll him toward the elevator.

"Bless him, Lord," she offers a whispered prayer. "And please, be close to me in this step I am about to take."

Inside the quarters identified "Director of Nursing" on the second floor, Dahlia's nervousness builds when she identifies herself to an assistant in the front office. She is thankful their voices are overheard and waiting time is eliminated.

"Please come in," Lori Hutchinson calls from the inner office.

Dahlia commands her legs to move toward the invitation. The superior who issued it remains seated at her desk. She offers a smile and a welcoming motion of hand for Dahlia to be seated. Two simple acts that put a bit of starch in Dahlia's wilted spirit.

"I've asked you here so that I may personally congratulate you on the progress I've noted from your latest weigh-in," the director says, "I see that you have lost another seven pounds. This tells me the recommended diet, and your willingness to work toward our common goals are moving in harmony. The committee has reviewed your profile, and we find that... upon re-evaluation of your height, overall body structure, and your most recent examinations...a revised target of one hundred ninety pounds seems appropriate to meet all standards. That means you'll need to lose another ten pounds. Do you think you can do it?"

Dahlia's ears stop working after the welcome sound of "one hundred ninety pounds." Her exultant "I'll do it, Miss Hutchinson," gushes forth. From Dahlia's present 200 pounds, a goal of 190 seems far more reachable than the first assigned target of 175.

Then second thoughts take hold. She has 10 pounds to go. Shedding each pound has become increasingly difficult.

The director sees the light go out of Dahlia's facial expression. "I'm sure it hasn't been easy," she says. Her own eyes reveal compassion.

"No, Ma'am, it's not easy," Dahlia sighs. "The last seven pounds were a struggle, I tell you. The first twenty pounds went pretty fast... but ever since... well, I follow my diet, and I keep active, still..."

Lori Hutchinson breaks the silence. "It's also been noted that your work performance has not suffered. You are to be commended for your dedication to your patients' well-being. We want you to continue as a member of our nursing staff. I believe an exception might be made in your next weigh-in target. If you are able to show and maintain a reduction of five pounds at the end of each of two consecutive months, we can all agree the goal has been met."

Dahlia's early rush of excitement revives at this news. Perhaps someone has read her mind, heard her cry for help, and though it seems as unlikely as frost in July, it is this person of authority.

"Then it will be a matter of your staying at that level," the director adds.

The solemn remark prompts Dahlia to respond in a similar tone. "Yes, Miss Hutchinson, that won't be easy either. I know that, but I feel like you want me to make it. That's the biggest helping hand I could wish for. I appreciate your trust. I won't let you down."

"That's all we ask."

More suggestions follow as the director concludes, but the words "one hundred ninety pounds," and "five pounds less each month" float through Dahlia's consciousness as she returns to her station. Her next target is the loss of five pounds. Not seven, nor 10.

In her joy, a line from an old hymn springs to mind. Enlivened, she hums it softly and thinks how the savings of energy can be spent on problems that await at home.

Once more, this time aloud, she hums "...and I know...He watches...me."

12

The Visitation

They came in pairs, in clusters, here and there a lone individual The line of friends paying last respects had moved in unbroken rhythm for more than an hour. That outpouring of concern energized Julia to stand near the open half of her husband's casket without excusing herself for even a minute. Her son Thad remained a constant presence at her left.

"I wish you would sit down, Mom," 36-year-old Thad whispered regularly. "Just a few minutes... no one will leave without speaking with you at one of the chairs over there." The large, well-appointed room offered both chair and couch seating among and in front of ornamental china cabinets and the dark wood writing desks that line the interiors of most funeral parlors.

"I'd rather be here, Thad," she whispered to him before greeting another member of the line.

Julia and Thad constituted the entire receiving corps since Thad's wife Elaine left a few minutes earlier with the three adolescent grandchildren of the late Ernest Walker. As morning anchorman, sports voice, and part owner of Radio 95.7 for 27 years, Ernie Walker became the area's best known personality – more identifiable than any mayor, police chief, or state lawmaker who held office during the same period. Word of his passing traveled swiftly from customer-to-server or server-to-customer at every eating place in town and wherever his longtime listeners gathered in retail stores, offices, and government buildings.

Julia reminded Thad of that notoriety when she insisted they receive friends in both afternoon and evening sessions. The two-hour afternoon block had been well attended; now the evening's attendance would likely double that number. Instead of feeling tired, Julia gained stamina from these expressions of affection for her husband.

Endearing, too, were the words repeated by what seemed like every third person in line, "It's an honor to meet 'Mrs. One and Only.'" Ernie's on-air reference to Julia grew popular with his listeners, and each day's broadcast included some wise saying he attributed to 'My One and Only' or, just as often, when she was the never-heard-from target of one of his pranks.

In a turn of head to receive the next attendee, Julia caught sight of Ernie's ex-business partner Harlan Shaw making his way into the room. Shaw, as general partner with 40 per cent control, made the decisions which resulted in Ernie's leaving the station. Thad stoutly took his father's side at the break-up, and Julia feared Shaw's presence here might be seen by her son as offensive.

She seized her first opportunity to whisper an alert. "Harlan just came in. Please, let's not have any unpleasantness."

Thad's response stoked her fear. "I don't want to talk to him, Mom."

Their whispered confidences continued between full-throated chats with others as the line advanced: Julia urged calm; Thad determined to avoid Shaw altogether.

Ernie Walker had owned 30 per cent of the radio station with the remaining 30 per cent controlled by Trust of Texas Bank. Ernie's expertise was programming and Shaw's was business, which made them an effective team for more than 20 years. The general partner had the greater authority, however. His influence brought the bank principals in line quickly when an opportunity arose to sell the station at a handsome profit. The new owner-ship switched overnight to a youth-centered sound with which they had success in other markets. That up-tempo format had no place for Ernie's folksiness. The onetime partners went separate ways, and neither attempted to contact the other after all terms were settled.

His sudden exile from the airwaves plunged Ernie into depression for a time. He did all right financially from the sale, but he missed the daily rapport with thousands of people he never met in person. Julia strove tirelessly to lift his spirits. Thad came up with the idea to set up a soundproof recording booth in the Walkers' basement. His wife and son kept prodding until Ernie consented to record commercial announcements for many of the same local businesses who once advertised on his program. The phrase 'My One and Only' found its way into more than one of his spiels as commercial spokesman for appliance stores and automobile dealerships. Invigorated anew, he branched into voiceover work for the local cable television system and, from that foothold, persuaded the cable owners to devote a channel for live coverage of high school football and basketball with Ernie describing play by play. The exile was short-lived.

As Shaw advanced toward their positions near the casket, Julia offered to exchange places with her son. "I'll speak first... you won't have to say much."

"I don't want to say anything at all," Thad murmured.

"Well, I might just go sit in one of those chairs over there," Julia teased. "Then you'll be alone, and you'll *have* to talk with him."

She felt her son's strong grip on her left arm. "Not now, Mom," he said, countermanding his own advice, "Please...let's see this through together." He accepted the change in positions without another word. They greeted another half dozen acquaintances before Shaw and a woman with him stood before them.

Shaw greeted her with an obvious try at warmth, "Julia, you get more beautiful every..." his voice lost verve.."time I see you." She wondered if he realized how hollow the words sounded since they had not seen each other for more than five years.

"Old Ernie was so fortunate to have found you," Shaw hurried to say. He sounded more sincere when he praised Ernie's contributions to their station's achievements. "You had so much to do with the energy he brought to work," he complimented. "You gave him balance." Before allowing Julia time to reply, the noticeably ill at ease Shaw introduced the smartly dressed, noticeably younger woman at his side. "I don't believe you've met my wife, Annie. We married year before last."

"Hello, Annie.. Hello, Harlan," she offered her hand first to the new wife, then to Shaw. "It's nice of you to come."

Shaw spoke in a nervous rush. "Well, of course I wanted to pay my respects to my old and dear friend Ernie... and to you, Julia. We went through so much together. Good times and bad. You witnessed it all, didn't you? I hadn't heard anything about... illness." A quizzical look accompanied the last words.

Julia saw that he expected details, but this was not a time for lengthy explanation with others waiting patiently. "It was a blood clot, Harlan. No warning. Do you remember our son, Thad?" She pulled Thad's elbow until he brushed against her side.

"Of course, of course," Shaw stammered. "He grew up running around our studios. May I offer my condolences, young man? And those of my wife, as well."

"Thank you, Mister Shaw... Mrs. Shaw," Thad said with a swift shake of Shaw's hand. He looked to Julia for support, but she had turned to the next couple in line. Thad forced himself to break the awkward pause and speak again.

"I'm sure Dad would want me to say that you honor him by your presence. As you see, his listeners never forgot him."

"Of course, of course," Shaw stammered.

Thad wished he would move on, but the man seemed immobilized with much he wanted to say if he could overcome his obvious embarrassment. At last the wife, to Thad's relief, stroked Shaw's arm and lifted the spell.

"I'm sorry the new owners... did not understand..." Shaw began but stalled.

Julia, aware that others were blocked from speaking to Thad, came to the rescue in time to overhear Shaw's last comment.

"Ernie went on with his life, Harlan," she said. "He filled it well... so should we all."

The ex-partner nodded. A surprisingly meek acquiescence, Thad thought, for such a once gregarious man. Still without words, Shaw left them and guided his wife to take up a position with him before the opened half of the casket.

Thad gave his attention to his mother's introduction of the next persons in line, but on the periphery he saw the Shaws leave the casket and head for the exit. Slumped shoulders within the man's expensive suit expressed more than his fumbling attempt to put feelings into words. But he found his voice once he recognized an acquaintance who waited near the door to speak to him. Missing, though, was the old Shaw composure and charm Thad saw as a boy.

Later, after the funeral director cleared the room for Julia and Thad to have a few final minutes with their loved one, Thad mentioned Shaw's departure.

"I think I felt sorry for him, Mom."

Julia squeezed her son's hand. "You're wise for your years, Thad. Harlan has prospered in every way except in knowing himself. The wife with him tonight is number three. Each one more expensive, so I've been told. What's the term? High maintenance? One who's known him for a long time... and I have... can see Harlan's financial success has not brought the satisfaction he gained from those early years with Ernie... when they built that station into a powerhouse."

Thad's free arm embraced her. "You would not let Dad sink into that pit of emptiness, Mom. I'll always thank you for that. I suppose I've looked at the visitation, or wake... whatever it's called, as a time when folks come to try and make the family feel better. I think Mister Shaw came tonight to try and make himself feel better. Do you think we helped him?"

"Only he knows, Thad. Perhaps he felt some comfort in the gracious way he was received. Be proud we did that for Ernie."

With her son's arm around her shoulder, Julia looked down at the still head at rest on a silk pillow.

"Good night, Mister One and Only," she said

Made in the USA
Lexington, KY
21 May 2015